Paint Dries as a Train Goes Off The Rails

Nicholas Marchuk

This book is dedicated to anyone that has played music for people that didn't care to hear it.

Contents

1

Vincent Reznor took a long, dry hit from his vape and closed his eyes. He clenched his jaw and felt his blood turn to molasses. The fish guts and dried blood caked onto his apron melted away, disappearing onto the pavement below. He could hear his knuckles turning white. A little tent formed in his jeans. Could life be any better? In a moment, the rush was over. He shivered, shook his head, and stuffed the vape in his pocket. His cousin always told him it was gay to vape, but it was cool to be gay now, so nobody cared if you vaped. He was living in the future.

The next thing he grabbed was the controller for his electric skateboard. He pushed forward on the remote, picking up speed as he passed through the back alley and out onto the main road. Another shift at the restaurant was behind him. He watched the ivy-laden brick rowhouses and vinyl triple-deckers fly by, remnants of the past and present. The sun was beating down overhead, and that was righteous as well. He tilted his head skyward. Maybe he'd catch a tan. Maybe Mack, the girl at the record store around the block, would let him hit on her break. Fuck yeah.

He took his phone from his pocket and shuffled the music he was listening to. It played some junk from a local band. He didn't love that stuff so much, but these were local guys, and it was important to support them. They might be stupid geeks who make bad art rock who should know their place and not fucking talk to his girl at the record store, but at least they were from around here. The chorus of this song was loud. The guitars crashed and burned together with the kick drum and the cymbals. Vincent liked loud.

A thought came to him about how he could make the moment even better. He pulled his vape from his pocket and ripped another long hit. "RAAAAAH!" he shouted, stretching his arms out wide, willing his board to go faster until the wheels shook and rattled. A shadow flashed at the edge of his perception.

The front wheels of his board jammed into the exposed rail of the train tracks that crossed the road before him. He flipped head over heels onto the gray cracked pavement ahead, smearing blood and dirt onto his apron. He gathered his wits, caught his breath. He'd gotten ahead of himself. That was alright, another scar to show Mack later. Maybe she'd wrap it up for him, and he'd say he was doing something brave. He'd gotten a serious burn on his back from the road, and he writhed on the pavement, trying to move past it. Then the sound of bells came.

The arm that blocks the railroad crossing was on its way down, the regular chiming of the bells announcing the arrival of a train. Vincent looked around to make sure he wasn't in its path. He saw he was a few feet beyond it. Okay, whatever. He breathed for a moment, then remembered his board. Where the hell was his board? If he could have made a list of his most prized possessions, the board probably came second on it after his vape. He saw it, still lying across the tracks, and it called to him. He reached his bloodied arm out at it, and that was when the train came. "My board!" he shouted, falling to his scraped knees, regretting it immediately. "Fuck, bro!" He fell back onto his back.

Squealing, a deafening crashing sound that seemed to never end. The sound of metal crunching and cracking and folding in on itself. The belching of black smoke and sparks flying. The sound of an old wooden building buckling and falling. The roar of the locomotive as it lay in a ditch, engine still running. The mile-long train had derailed, each successive car being thrown off the tracks and forced into nearby buildings and cars and each other. Vincent felt white-hot metal chunks being thrown at him, burning him, biting at his skin and his clothes. He crawled in reverse, unable to look away from the explosion. What had he done? The twisted rail cars built up until the train could go no further. The last car ground to a halt in the middle of the road, the place he'd just crossed now impassable.

A raven flew overhead, fleeing all that he had wrought. He coughed on the dust that had been kicked around and watched it settle. His apron had turned shades of brown and red. Probably needed a new one; the chef wouldn't like that. This whole situation was bananas. Mack was never gonna believe it. Things were quiet otherwise. He heard what sounded like a campfire, crackling, burning near him. From near the locomotive, a plume of smoke shot hundreds of feet in the air, an eruption beyond description, raining fire and ash down on the place that was kind of nowhere. It was a plume of red and orange from hell itself, bloody and angry and punishing. He saw the raven fall from the sky, its wings beating weakly against the smoke but unable to stay airborne. It fell to the ground by him, where it lay dead. And then a sickness not unlike sleep took him.

2

Connor let his bicycle skid to a stop in the hard gravel on the side of the road. At the edge of the forest, he leaned it against a tree. The job site, which he and his fellow painters had been toiling at for several days, was an aging rail bridge, just outside of town. Several metal trusses with wide support columns were bolted into concrete blocks, set deep into the earth. The metal on the old bridge had begun to rust, and already the off-white chipped paint had run red.

He and his friends painted exteriors for a living. Today, their task was to restore the white finish of the bridge, paint over any graffiti they found in the area, and stay out of trouble. The area was an artificial valley where the railroad had dug through a hill, leaving steep stone retaining walls on either side. He rumbled down the slope of the hill and ducked under a low branch, revealing the site. Three men were already up on ladders and working. Two of them were his closest friends, Nigel and Pablo. They were 'adoptive' twin brothers as they liked to say, with no relation that Connor knew about. The third was Stirbert, who he liked, but was less close to. Probably on account of him being the son of his boss.

"Cheers, Connor," Nigel said, leaning off the side of his ladder and waving his brush. "How ya been?"

"Nothing at all, man," Connor replied. Nigel was a British fellow, about thirty, friendly in the face, balding, with an even temperament. It was strange that he ended up here. Pablo also shouted a greeting but was too busy bending in an awkward position, trying to reach a difficult corner. Connor picked up a nearly full bucket of paint from the ground and pried the lid off. He dipped his finger in the mixture and watched it drip back into the bucket. As a child, he'd always had a non-serious urge to taste the thick, sticky paint, just because the texture seemed appealing. Now the idea made him rightfully sick, but the texture still appealed to him.

He set his backpack on the ground and removed a speaker, queuing the first few songs of the day on his phone. It wasn't his preference to stick with an album or a playlist, instead choosing the right songs manually for every moment. He hit play and got to work.

"Man, I like this one!" Pablo said, coming uncurled from the awkward position he was in. "This shit is junk!"

It was junk. Junk was the name of an up-and-coming musical style that was born in their small town and had begun to spread. It started when a few Ohioan transplants took their emo musical traditions to the winding rivers and bucolic rolling hills of New Jersey, and mixed it with the local style. The result was music that was at times egregiously loud, and at other times only moderately loud, with doses of yearning and longing. The music was incredibly unpopular with people over thirty-five. The legend was that at one point, a sorry Gen X-er had referred to it as 'junk music', and the name had stuck. Now the popular thing was to say the opposite of what you meant. Calling a song junk, trash, filthy, or even stinky, was the highest compliment.

When Connor first started, he had wondered if he would struggle to get recognition from the other painters. While they had all grown close by now, he was nervous at the time. He sought to impress them with his music taste. Neither Pablo nor Nigel were from the area in the way that Connor was, and so they didn't know as much about Junk. When they'd given him a chance on aux, he'd taken a risk and played that music. It turned out that music that civilized adults found grating was perfect background music for painters with one or two screws loose. When they weren't rocking out to Junk, the conversation flowed easily. Nigel was a natural conversationalist, patient but also able to contribute in his own right.

"500 upstrokes for my new post!" Nigel exclaimed, as he checked his phone. With his other hand, he wiped paint on his coveralls. Nigel was the only one left of them with social media, but he had a quirky way of going about it: He'd found an app specifically for painters. The verification process was arduous, and it involved submitting several photos showing you next to something you'd painted, which were manually reviewed by moderators. Pablo had been helping Nigel put together an application when Connor first started working there.

"Give me that," Connor said, hopping down from his ladder. He took the phone from Nigel's hand. "Let's see what the old man has to say."

"Every crew has that one guy named Nigel," he read aloud. "Then there are several laughing emojis." There were indeed 500 upstrokes on the post, and twenty-five 'repaints', as it were.

Nigel tried to swipe his phone back, but Connor dodged him. "C'mon, that's too easy!" Connor laughed. "They don't know that's you. Get outta here."

"Lying on the internet," Pablo muttered. "Sad to see what my brother has come to."

"No lying was involved," Nigel explained, finally getting his phone back from Connor. He stuffed it in his breast pocket. "And all good writers write what they know. Even a child knows that."

Nigel returned to his crevice. "A child, yes. Even Stirbert," Pablo said, laughing. The guys had been teasing Stirbert all day, and he was taking it well, though he hadn't piped up very often. He was still learning the ins and outs of the job, and was a little younger than the rest of them, still in college.

Painting was not a hard job, at least to Connor, since the work didn't command a lot of technical accuracy. Connor had started to find that the more he painted, he could see differences in how professional and amateur jobs looked. There was something about the evenness of well-applied strokes and the care with which the more talented painters (like Pablo) could cover even the most forgotten corners of a surface. It was satisfying to watch, and more satisfying to experience himself.

Before long, it was lunchtime, and they sat on various medium-sized boulders by the tracks to eat their packed lunches. Connor had made himself an egg salad sandwich that morning, light on the mayonnaise and heavy on the mustard, the opposite of how his parents preferred it. The four of them all cracked open a Boom, the local energy drink everyone in town seemed to drink.

It was then that he heard the breaking of twigs and footsteps up on top of the hill, behind the trees. They came in groups of three, like whoever was out there was alternately running and then catching themselves from falling. He saw the feet of the mysterious runner first, as they approached the low branch. A moment later, they collided head-first with the low branch and fell backward to the ground. They rolled down the hill, bouncing a few times, before landing on the gravel by the train tracks.

"Ow, fuck!" the woman's voice shouted. On the ground was a girl about Connor's age, wearing ill-fitting denim overalls, now stained by the dirt and gravel from her tumble. She wore black work boots with yellow laces, and a tie-dyed undershirt. Her black hair was cut a little above her shoulders. Pablo was already over to help her to her feet.

"Another new hire?" Pablo smiled. He checked to see if she was alright.

"Yeah," she said, rubbing her forehead where it had contacted the branch. "For now."

Connor had had no idea that a new person would be coming along that day. He reached out his hand to shake hers. "Connor," he said.

She stretched out her arm to meet his, and their eyes met. "Connor," she said, as if testing the name out. "I'm Kara." She squeezed his hand once, not shaking it, the handshake of someone who was rarely invited to shake hands. He studied her face for the half-second it took to let her hand go. A smirk, or maybe a half-smirk, like the Mona Lisa. An expression that you could write a thinkpiece about what it meant. There was not much to say about her outfit, other than that it worked in her favor. It seemed like she might take care of her eyebrows. After categorizing all that information, processing it, and returning to reality, he realized what it meant—he found her attractive.

He grabbed a spare brush and handed it to her. "Shall we?" he asked.

"Sure," she said, dusting her pants off. "Let's try this."

He had her follow him to where he had been working. He dipped the brush into the paint and watched it drip back into the bucket. "So, this isn't a hard job," he said. "It's an easy job. You can't do it wrong. We just have to cover the entire surface in a single color. Just like, make it look new again. But still, what's worth not doing wrong is worth doing right."

"I don't think I've heard that one before," she replied. She squinted at the paintbrush he'd given her. "Did you make it up?"

"Isn't everything made up?" Connor said. That answer was good enough. Maybe he'd made it up, he couldn't be sure. Maybe, more accurately, the words had appeared on the tip of his tongue, and he'd spat them out without realizing it. He looked up at the rusted metal beam and began to paint, and she watched him intently.

He instructed her to try a little on her own and returned to his work. The darkened white of the existing paint had flaked off in pieces, and larger wafers in spots. Many things were flat—fake hardwood floors, computer screens, the sky. Rust was different. He could look at a bit of a rusted bridge for an hour and not run out of things to see in it. Streaks of red iron ran down the metal beam like tears, staining the concrete blocks below before disappearing into the gravel and weeds.

"Everything requires maintenance," he said, working as he spoke. "Except for nature. That goes on its own. You have to do stuff like this to keep the world turning."

A red chip got stuck in his brush. "See," he said. "A straggler." He shook it out of the brush. "These bits don't matter, but I don't like when they get in the bucket.

"Okay," she said. "Am I doing it right?"

He looked. She'd covered a few square feet of beam in white paint. No drips on the ground, or missed spots. The brushwork was even and parallel. The divots in the beam had been carefully covered, but not filled with paint.

"Kara," he said. "Are you an artist?"

"I draw," she said, chuckling a little. "Who doesn't draw?"

Connor didn't draw. He blinked. "This is great," he said, feeling the ears of his coworkers perking up as he said so. "Well, uh, some things here and there of course. You'll pick it up with time. There will have to be some more training."

She nodded politely, and started again, further down the beam.

"There's one thing, though," Connor said. "Before all that paint dries. You'll want to leave your mark now, since the part you did is around eye level. Easier to see."

"My mark?" she asked. "I don't know. Isn't it a little crude to sign your name like this/ Like a kid sticking their hand in wet concrete?"

"Nothing so crude," he replied. "Look here," he said, pointing up at a higher portion of the beam. From a distance, it was just plain white, but on closer inspection, the brush strokes made a swirling pattern, with a little extra paint, enough for the form to reveal itself in the right light.

"Do you see it? The trick is to do it all in one stroke."

"Oh, yes!" she said, standing on her tiptoes to see better. "That's pretty rad. I see what you mean, though. Let me think."

She removed a pocketknife from her pants and unsheathed it, looking at the blade for a moment. She walked up to the beam, so close that he thought her nose may accidentally touch the paint. From his vantage point, it was hard to tell what she was doing, but she was meticulously cutting at the paint, scraping it, spreading it. She wiped the knife on her pants. She picked up a piece of rust that had flaked on the ground and crushed it between her fingers. It stained them red. She gently mixed the powder into the drying paint where she'd been working and spread it around until it was a warmer shade of white.

After some last adjustments, she stepped back. "There. I'm done." The white color of the beam now had a square inlaid in it, of a warmer, darker shade of white, barely noticeable if you weren't looking directly at it. The square was rotated slightly as if one of its corners was being lifted from the ground. The border between the broad strokes of the painting around it, and the refined surface of the square was crisp. It held his attention for some reason.

"Did you come up with this?" he asked.

"No," she said, starting to paint again in another spot. She seemed eager to work. "Malevich, an old painter. It's his work, White on White, it's called. You know, from around when it was cool to just paint shapes. It was edgy and cool to throw a shape out there and call it art. Malevich, he at least had some reasons for It. He was upset that art had too much to do with the material world. Lots of things were happening, during his time. He wanted the form of the art to be supreme, above the material."

Connor thought for a moment. "And you being here today, putting his square on this beam, saying it's yours, how's that work? Would he be upset?"

She turned her head towards his and grinned. "Well, he didn't want it to mean anything, you know, in the real world. Form only. To me, he may as well have put it in the public domain. So maybe it's mine." She put her brush down and pulled the hair off the back of her neck. Tattooed there was a square, rotated a few degrees to the right.

A slow rumble came from beneath them. A paint bucket resting on a railroad tie began rattling in place. "Train!" Nigel shouted, hopping down from his ladder. The men made quick work of moving their equipment to safety. Connor grabbed the bucket and the brush Kara had set down. Kara started up the embankment, as the train horn started to blare. The conductor seemed angry today.

"No!" he shouted. "Here!" he pointed beside him. He leaned against the stone wall that was just feet from the edge of the tracks. Kara shrugged, and hopped back down the hill, walking over to stand beside him. Nigel, Pablo, and Stirbert stood on the other side.

The train's horn cried louder and louder as it approached. Black birds flew from the nearby trees. The engineers hated people on the tracks. Connor shut his eyes and turned his head to the right, not wanting to see it approach. He dug his nails into the bricks as the rumbling grew louder, the anticipation unbearable. Why they did this to themselves he could never explain. Kara shrank further against the wall and then looked left. Not to him, but past him, staring down the moving train. A moment passed and the train was upon them, car after car hurtling by. The wind revealed the black square on her neck. Another moment passed and it was gone.

3

The painters sat around a table at the Stinky Rat, a twenty-four-hour diner in town. "Welcome," Pablo said, as the waitress placed a milkshake in front of Kara.

"Every painter who does honest work is entitled to an honest milkshake, at the end of the day."

"It's an old tradition," Nigel said. "It's said that the painters who once worked on the Roman aqueducts would eat grapes at the end of the day. Not nearly as delectable, but the sentiment is similar."

"Grapes?" Pablo asked.

"They had grapes in Rome. I'm sure of it."

"Either way," Pablo said, waving off Nigel's comments. "This is a most honorable and fitting treat for a worker such as yourself. They see you with a drink like this, and they know you put in an honest day's work." He grinned.

"Where'd you learn words like that, Pablo? Honorable and fitting?" Nigel asked.

"The thing they say about becoming wise, is that it happens when you least expect it. Perhaps I became wise right when I walked in the door this morning—maybe it was last week. Who can know? I'm wise enough to defer judgment on the subject." They all laughed at that.

Connor watched as Kara's eyes scanned the restaurant, as he took a long sip of his drink. It was relatively well-attended, for it being 8 o'clock on a weeknight. The walls were painted crimson and had photos framed of various politicians shaking hands with the waitstaff hung up. Some guitars, signed with unreadable signatures, hung from the ceiling near the bar, which was built of the vernacular corrugated metal known to be used in an archetypal diner.

"So, Kara," Nigel said.

"New girl," Pablo added.

"Yeah, quite new," she said.

"What's your story?" he asked. "How'd you end up somewhere like this? This place is kind of nowhere."

"Seems like a nice restaurant," she said, smirking. Connor thought she glanced at him for a second.

"Yeah, she's got a point," Connor said.

"But really—" Pablo said. "—what's this place got to do with you?"

She stirred her milkshake and looked out at the window. A car hummed by. "I'm from two towns over."

"How do you reckon?" Nigel asked.

"Well, this place is Kind of Nowhere. Down the main road, there's Someplace Else, and then if you head north a little ways, that's where I'm from. Way Out There."

"Is that near Somewhere?" Stirbert asked. He was from Somewhere, so of course he'd ask that.

"They had a petition to rename it Getting Somewhere, but it never caught on," she said. "Anyway, you know, growing up there was fine. I have nothing to report on that end. It's just slow there. My mom and dad get along fine, they are together still. I have an older brother, but he's a bit older, so we don't talk much. I don't know what else to say. My name is Kara, I have a degree in planning from the school that's near here, and a fun fact about me is... I'm very flexible!"

"Flexible! That's a boring one."

"Please don't demonstrate," Stirbert added.

"Planning, how's that?" Connor asked. He had an idea, but he liked her manner of speaking. It was refreshing to have someone new to question.

"Well, it's a bit like plotting, less like scheming, though there's some common ancestry to them," she said, laughing.

"Oh," Connor said. He wasn't sure what to say to that. "Alright."

"But you're not planning, right now?" Pablo asked.

"No plans," she said. Her milkshake was nearly empty now, and it had only been minutes since she'd gotten it. "New job, new town. New crew. That's my plan right now, to get used to all of that. I wanted to have a job planning, but it didn't work out."

"It's good to work," Pablo said. "That much is true. So, I commend you for playing your part in society." He had this habit of offering comments that sounded like advice but were really just statements.

"I don't know," she said. "It's good that we can take care of columns, walls, whatever needs taking care of. But is it art?"

"Why's it matter if it's art?" Stirbert asked, frowning. "It's got to be done."

"No, she's right," Pablo said. "It's good that you are confronting this so early. Your mind, Stirbert, is too focused on... the checks, the bills. Numbers that go in and out, up and down. As workers, we should evaluate our place in the machine, what role we play."

"And if you're so smart, then what's it all mean?" Kara smirked. "What's the answer?"

"Meaning, yes. Say we all say tomorrow, that we won't paint the bridge. Maybe someone else comes and paints the beams. Maybe not. Maybe I work for less so I can paint bridges and things we need instead of painting bombs red at the bomb factory. Maybe I go into painting because I think being a real estate agent—which I would be very good at, mind you—is unethical. But art? There is no art in it. We're getting paid! We sold out, maybe. Say for example that tomorrow I don't feel creative, I don't have any inspiration to make art. The dream, it escapes me for a moment. Still, I need money, so I show up tomorrow and paint something awful. I have not created art. It is the destruction of art. If I knew French, I'd say a terrible and beautiful French phrase that summed it all up."

"Mise en place," Stirbert said, solemnly.

"Yes!" Pablo said, thrusting his open hand towards Stirbert. "The boy is right. Mise en place. Perfect."

"Meaning without art," she said. "Okay, I'll have to think about that."

The sound of a guitar broke the flow of their conversation. Over at the back wall was a small stage raised a foot above the ground, and a band had set up. Droning tones sounded through the restaurant as they began to tune.

"Whoa," Kara said. "Live music?"

"It never ends," Pablo said, rubbing his forehead. "No, it's good, it's good. But it never ends. Truly. There is music all the time."

Kara nodded happily. "Pretty cool right?" Connor said. "The guitarist is my buddy from high school." He pointed at a flannel-wearing man frowning at an amp.

"Wow," she said. "You play guitar?"

"No," he said, which was the truth. "But I think that like, my conversations with him might inform his playing. Inspiration, you know. Something like that."

Connor remembered a late night at his friend's mom's house. He was playing some guitar solo for Connor, hammering on, pulling off, traipsing along the pentatonic scale with ease, playing as many notes as he pleased. He'd asked Connor what he thought about it after. Connor had said that it was good, but it didn't seem like he was playing for any good reason. Just playing for the sake of it. That comment had made things awkward for a bit.

"That makes sense," she said. The band started to play, and she turned in her seat to watch.

And now we ride the circus wheel
And it's your brother's favorite wheel
He says it's good to ride a wheel
But now he's dead and can't ride the wheel
The Earth looks better on a screen

Than it does on amphetamines
He didn't think that you would cry
When he rode the wheel with another guy
The circus can really break your heart
The way they treat those elephants is not art

Nigel turned back to face the group. "Not sure what that one is about," he said.

"It's a classic," Connor said. "They are covering a song, by the Last Actuaries. They are some of the fathers of Junk music. Everything changed when this song came out."

"Yeah, the part where he rides a Ferris wheel moved me," Nigel said, sarcastically.

Connor listened to the song as they went over the chorus again. "It's a sad song," he noted.

"What happened to that band?" Kara said. "Can we see them live?"

Nigel made a face, and Pablo did too. Stirbert laughed as well. "They, uh, did some bad things," Connor said. "You know how it is. Nobody likes to talk much about it. Maybe that's a flaw on our part."

"That's nice," she said, tapping her straw in her empty glass. "That's nice."

Pablo stood. "I've got some things to take care of back at home."

Nigel stood as well. "I was going to lay in bed," he said. "But I'll head out as well. Shall we?"

They walked from the restaurant out onto the street. They all lived in or around the west end of town, the denser, older part of the city. The street grid seemed to predate the invention of the grid. People said that they were former cattle paths. Some roads were only ten feet wide, not enough to drive a vehicle down, paved with cobblestones that were sinking more and more with time. The sidewalks were brick, as were the buildings. They were old, three stories high, usually, and they leaned. They leaned over the road, away from it, and the narrowness of the road amplified that feeling. The canyons, some people called it.

They continued their journey down the road before turning down an alleyway. This one had concrete walls, which were painted with graffiti. The tags blended into one another, a sea of neon colors, some faded, and some fresh. A rat scuttled under a hole in the low part of the wall. They scooted past where a row of city trash cans were

"This is so cool," Kara said. "I need to get out here more often."

"We like it. It's ours," Pablo said. "Well, it belongs to the community."

"You could add something, sometime," Connor said. "Maybe not during the day."

"That would be nice," she replied.

The first stop was near the end of the alley, a hallway cut into the concrete, a door at the end of it. Pablo had to duck his head to go down the hallway. He made his way to the red door, turned around, and saluted, before ducking inside. The others wished him well as he left.

They passed back onto a wider street, with more stately buildings and a couple of chain stores. The main grocery store was on this road, but it was a locally owned joint, the kind where things were just too expensive to shop there every day. It was the kind of place you'd go if you ran out of eggs in the middle of making pancakes. Everyone liked and respected the owner, a plump man of about forty who was a generational citizen of the neighborhood, but not enough to avoid the supermarket outside town for groceries, when they could.

Stirbert's apartment was on this road. A brownstone, white in color, the masonry aged yellow with time, crawling with green vines. A dog was tied up outside to the fence, and it scowled and howled at Stirbert as he walked up. Pablo had joked once that it was as if the dog knew that Stirbert had a silly name. The gang stood at a distance as he approached. The dog strained at the end of its leash, an old bully, brown and snarling. He performed the same feat every time, waiting until he got to the end of the dog's radius, before dashing down the path to the front door of his building, where the dog couldn't reach him. He waved with one hand as he ducked inside, safe. This act always amused them.

They walked more and passed a homeless man in a wheelchair. They didn't know his name and had never asked for it. They believed he lived in some form of public housing. He sat in his chair, banging a cup of change against the armrest.

He had taken to setting a beat with the banging of his cup, something simple and syncopated. They appreciated the music, so they'd give him a dollar when they had one, placing it in his cup.

"Isn't that guy wearing Jordans? He needs our money?" Kara asked after she watched Connor give him change.

"Yeah, he's cool," Connor said.

"He's a top lad," Nigel added. The Britishism was well met by Connor.

Nigel was next. He lived closer to the edge of the neighborhood, in a three-floor building with vinyl siding. To enter, he would scamper up a set of wooden stairs inelegantly added to the front of the building, when it had been converted to apartments. During the winter, it could be treacherous, and Nigel's landlord was a useless creep, who couldn't be bothered to have someone clean the snow. They often joked that Nigel was just waiting for a slip and fall that would result in an inevitable lawsuit.

Connor and Kara were the last, standing out on the sidewalk together. She said she lived close, but Connor insisted he walk her home. Down the street, he pointed out a building to her, a friendly duplex tucked between two larger buildings. It seemed in need of a fresh coat of paint, and a new roof.

"What, we're gonna paint it?" she asked.

"No, this one is called The Kingdom of Joy. It looks like a regular house during the day, which it is. But at night, the basement is the coolest place to be in. It gets loud."

"Really?" she asked. "That's so cool."

"Yeah. You have to be insanely good to get to play a show there. And know the right people. Especially know the right people, it seems, lately. It's too bad. Things have gotten so competitive."

"I love stuff like that," she said. "I had no idea that was here. Would you ever show me?"

Connor's heart skipped. "Yeah, we can go. I think there's a show in a couple of days. Nigel's cousin plays in the band—we can definitely get in."

She nodded happily. "That would be great. I'm excited."

4

Connor woke up and checked the time. Nine in the morning. Later than he'd wanted to get up. On days he didn't work, he tried to wake up with the light. It was darker than it should have been. At nine, the light should have been streaming into his room by now, casting a kind glow onto his few possessions. He walked over to the window. A layer of what seemed like soot covered it, like a thin film. He opened the window, an old wooden window that looked almost painted shut. He rubbed his finger on the outside part of the glass. The soot stained his finger, the same as if he'd dipped it in a pot of ink. He touched his tongue to the soot. Something had burned.

He checked his phone, sleep still pulling at him. Officials urge evacuation after massive train derailment causes explosion. He flipped to the group chat. Kara had been recently added. "This is for sure a Boom moment," Pablo had written. That told him little about what had happened. It was crass, but this situation, whatever it was, did call for an energy drink. He pulled the case of Boom out from under his bed and wriggled a can out of the plastic wrapping. He felt the liquid fuel collide with his stomach acid. Wow, he thought. That was the stuff.

He set his drink down and sat on the bed to pull a pair of cargo shorts on. These were his day-off shorts, ones that didn't have paint on them. As he was picking out some socks, a knock came at his front door. He made sure the top button of his pants was buttoned and shuffled over to see. Looking through the peephole, he saw a man in a polo, khakis, and a safety vest, holding a thick vanilla-colored folder and a clipboard.

"Hey uh," Connor said, opening the door. "What can I do you for?"

"I'm Mark Geilich from the Environmental Protection Agency," he said, not looking up from his clipboard. "As a precautionary measure, all residents living within three-quarters of a mile of the cleanup site are required to move to temporary housing while investigators determine whether your residence is safe for habitation. Do you have any questions?" He looked up at Connor without moving his head and smiled a friendly Kubrick stare.

"I guess that all makes sense to me," Connor said. "But what even happened?"

The man pulled a packet from his folder and handed it to Connor. It was titled There was a huge explosion near your home: Here's Why That Matters. "This packet should explain everything," he said. He then flipped a few pages into his own packet. "The EPA is also contracting with local content creators with an environmental justice background to make an explainer video. A copy will be delivered to your hotel room once the competitive bidding process is complete and the video is produced."

Connor flipped through the packet. Certain pages that didn't apply were crossed out, like the page for terrorist attacks. Well, at least it wasn't that. "Yeah, I guess an explainer will be helpful. And this packet should be useful. This is quite surprising."

"Is that an expression of shock or one of sadness?" the man asked. "If it's sadness I'm supposed to give you a hug."

"A hug?" Connor said. That was kind.

"Yeah you know what big guy, come here," the man said, embracing him.

"Okay... okay," Connor muttered, pushing him away after a moment. "Thanks, I guess."

"Yeah you know, just gotta follow the rules, ha," he said. "Didn't want to have to explain to my boss why I hadn't hugged anyone today. It would be impossible after a disaster of this scale for nobody on my route to want a hug. Questions would be asked."

"Improbable," Connor said. "I think you meant improbable, not impossible."

"Okay, where were we..." the man said. "Do you have any pets? Does anyone else live with you?"

"Just me."

"Are there any gender identities you'd feel uncomfortable sharing a hotel room with for up to six months?" he asked.

"Six months?" Connor yelped. "Are you serious?".

"Think of it like an upper bound on your little vacation," the man said. "The last time something like this happened, we had everyone back in two weeks. That was for the buildings that weren't demolished. I'll need you to answer the question though."

"I don't care," Connor said. "But can't I just have my own room? I mean, I like my setup."

He shook his head. "Not unless you have a doctor's note. We aren't made of money."

"Is my place gonna get demolished?"

"That won't be up to me. Seeing as you're here right now and you have four walls, I would say it's unlikely. However, your information packet has some statistics for your review. Based on how far you are from the explosion, you can estimate what kind of damage you or your home has sustained."

"Well, seems like you guys covered everything," Connor said. His stomach was starting to drop. What had happened?

"We covered everything, except for the cause of the explosion. But you know, fingers crossed!" the man gave him a thumbs up. Connor noted that he seemed to have significantly loosened up during the conversation. Good for him— talking to strangers was never easy.

It was evening by the time Connor hauled the last of his bags into the hotel room. He'd grabbed everything he could carry, and then some, not sure what was important, and what wasn't. He wouldn't lose his home, would he? That wouldn't make any sense. Things like that didn't just happen. He kicked the door shut. The move back would probably be no easier, but he pushed that thought from his mind. He flopped down on the queen size bed and rubbed his forehead. His arms and legs were sore.

"Hey idiot," came a voice from his right. "Gonna say anything yet?" It was Kara, lounging on the other bed in the room.

"What the hell?" Connor said, sitting up quickly. "What are you doing here? When did you get here?"

"You've been ignoring me for twenty minutes," she said, laughing. "We're roommates."

"Roommates," he said, rubbing his eyes. This was ridiculous. "That's cool with me, I guess."

"Well, I'm glad I have your permission," she said, picking up a book from the nightstand and removing the bookmark from it. She had the covers of the bed pulled down, with just her feet tucked under the sheets.

Connor walked over to the hotel room window. The hotel rose a few floors above the rows of triple-deckers rolling away into the forest. The sun was just somewhere out of his sight, but the street trees threw shadows on the buildings that waved and shook in the afternoon breeze. "View isn't bad," he said.

What he didn't say was what he saw out the window, beyond the houses, beyond the forest. A field of ash and fire. Smoke rising and disappearing into a white summer cloud.. The sickness grew in him, and it made his head ache. He leaned against the windowsill. He'd started to put the pieces together. He knew where the tracks crossed. Right through the edge of the neighborhood. What had been lost?

"I think there used to be a baseball field here. I'm pretty sure. Before it was a hotel."

"Really?" she said, interested.

Kids laughing, chasing each other in the outfield. The ping of the metal bat as adults sat around drinking and playing slow pitch. "My grandfather used to take me walking around here," he said. A blue button-up shirt tucked into a pair of pants that didn't fit. A warm calloused hand leading his own down the sidewalk. "I never played any baseball or anything like that. But my grandfather, we'd walk by and there was always a game going on, and he would say—I don't know a lick about baseball, but listen to me. When you're going through life, people will always tell you to keep your eye on the ball. Well, look at me now, I'm old as shit. What's my secret? Keep your eye on the bat, son. Keep your eye on the bat."

He turned and looked at Kara. She was leaning over in bed, watching him as he watched the window. "Keep your eye on the bat," she said. "I'll have to remember that one."

5

The next day they went to work. They weren't sure that they'd be paid, or that that was what they were supposed to do. Stirbert couldn't get a hold of his dad—he said he was too busy with cleaning up other messes to talk. Connor had been leaning towards not going. He was worried they might cross a police line or otherwise get in trouble. There had been swarms of vans, agencies, and other organs of government he hadn't heard of. Gruff people in hazmat suits were in sandwich shops taking their lunch breaks. Journalists were checking into local hotels and motels, and doing their writing in the shops that were still open.

The whole thing was a recipe for making Connor stay inside—but Kara had wanted to go, and so he went. She said they'd all have a 'mini therapy session' about the event, talk it over, and begin to process it. They walked together down the sidewalk in town. This portion of the city had handsome mill buildings, of red brick and large rounded windows that were beautiful but not energy efficient. They were passing the largest mill building in town, the Main Street Mill, which people said was nearly a mile long. Once the site of a booming textile industry, it has since been carved into restaurants, apartments, wedding venues, and various small businesses. There was even an art gallery, but he'd never been.

"It's nice here," Kara said. Connor agreed. Bricks were calming; they were an honest material for a building to be made of. He could envision that someone, at some point, had to stack each brick, one at a time. There was a human element to it.

They passed a coffee shop. "My buddy works here," Connor added. "We can get a free cup here sometime."

"A coffee hookup?" she laughed. "I'm impressed." A few adults were sitting at too-small tables out on the patio, plucking at their laptops.

"We'll turn here," Connor said, stepping out into the crosswalk. He jumped back as a car flew by, ignoring his imposition into the road. It passed only a foot from him. He stood, dazed, for a moment.

"Connor!" Kara shouted. He looked left and saw another car barreling towards him. Weird. He thought it had been slowing down. The tires screeched, and the car skidded to a halt, inches from his knee. He looked down at the car's matte black bumper, and blue hood, and up at the driver, a woman of middle age.

He raised both his hands. "Watch where you're going, lady!" Kara shouted as they started to leave.

The driver rolled her window down. Connor prepared for obscenities to be hurled at him, but instead, she hissed. A line of drool rolled down her chin, her fingers gripping the steering wheel, bony and pale. It was the kind of sound you didn't think a human could or should make. He felt a pull at his elbow as Kara pulled him back. A car whizzed by in the other direction, horn blaring.

"Come on," she said, tugging at his arm. "Let's get out of here. She's crazy."

"Yeah, let's go," he said, breathing heavily.

"Are you okay?"

"Just splendid," he said. He felt sick. Everything had been fine, a nice morning and a nice conversation, and then it was like he'd been doused in water. He could have vomited. He missed his apartment. The hotel room was both dingy and brightly lit, strange and clean. He could never get too comfortable. Comfort would always fool him, until fate pulled him away again. He pushed the thought away. No, this was just some weird lady. And roads were dangerous anyway, he should be careful. He should have been more careful. He should resume having a nice morning. Plus, even if he'd gotten hit, he'd roll over the windshield, and be uninjured anyways.

"You gonna say anything, or—?" Kara asked. "You're the one that knows the way."

"Right." He led her to the place where the buildings gave way to trees, but the road continued. The sidewalk turned to a gravel path beside the road. He lifted a tree branch, showing her the shortcut through the forest.

"Here, I'll say something, since you're so quiet," Kara said, ducking under the branch. "Are we at the point that I can tell you things?"

"Sure."

"Okay, that was a silly question. Anyways—do you ever wonder why you do normal stuff? Why you gotta do all this stuff, just to feel normal. You have to go outside, go for walks, eat right, or else your brain starts flickering? Things get all weird? It's unfair to have to do all that."

"Not sure. That's like, normal and shit. That's why I do it. I am walking right now, 'cause that's how I go to work. I'm outside because I'm not inside. That's how I live. I'm not really disappointed in that."

She sighed. "It's just, when you have a dog—the dog doesn't take itself out, you take it out."

"Or it pees on the floor."

"Yeah, it pees on the floor. But you have to go take it out, you have to feed it. Dogs are a whole project; it's why I don't have one here, even though I'd love one. I realized that I'm the same project. I have to take myself out for walks, and for what? Nobody's going to take me out if I don't leave my apartment for a few days. Everyone would be mad if I was at the convenience store and peed on the floor. Not that I'd do that."

"Yeah, I guess I never thought about it that way," Connor said. "I don't really worry about that stuff. Maybe I'll remind you to go for walks if you need me to."

"Very funny," she laughed. "If I catch you taking me out for walks, you're screwed."

"Too late," he said, kneeling down to pick up a large rock. He threw it and watched it glance off a tree trunk, frightening a squirrel. "But yeah, I mean, I get it. It's crazy you gotta deal with all that, I guess. If I wasn't working, I'd probably walk a lot less."

"I guess that's a good enough lesson."

They heard the voices of their comrades as they crested the last hill. Nigel, Pablo, and Stirbert were not down at the construction site; they were sitting up on the bridge, in a row, chatting idly.

"Look who it is!" Nigel said as they approached.

"What's up?"

"Hey, you guys alright?" Kara asked. "Like, is everyone's family okay?"

"It's all cheery," Pablo said. "I've only lost my house. I was lucky I was up, having a dark, brooding evening in my bedroom. I heard the commotion, and had the presence of mind to leave before the fire came for me."

"That's really scary," Connor said. He'd always liked Pablo's place.

"My twin's going to take me in, isn't that right Nigel?"

"Happy to do it, brother," Nigel said, giving Connor a pleading look. "We'll be roommates for a bit."

Pablo wasn't finished speaking. "But as for what's wrong—well, what could be wrong in the world? It's hard to say. You know, there is hunger and poverty all around, but that's all abstract. This time, the suffering is not abstract at all. You only need to look up."

Pablo motioned out at the vista before him. Connor was confused at first but knew immediately when he looked. It was like nothing he'd seen before, except maybe once on the news—acres of burnt forest, brunt buildings, broken and blackened. It seemed to have been the west end of town that had borne the brunt of the damage. Their neighborhood. Now, half of it seemed to be gone. There was no neighborhood, only a crater. Half-burnt and half-fallen buildings spilled their guts out onto the ground, covered in a thick layer of gray dust. In the center of it all, there were dozens of railcars, twisted and melted together, stained black from the flames. There were fire trucks, with tiny firefighters shooting water on still-smoking piles of debris.

"Pretty gnarly," Nigel said. "I'm just glad we're, you know, far away from it. And I'm glad we escaped with our lives, of course."

"It's a total mess," Stirbert said. "How do you even begin to clean that up? It's like one big pile of trash."

"Someone will," Pablo said. "And that person will get paid handsomely."

"Do they know what happened?" Kara asked. She pulled a croissant from her backpack and began to chew.

"Someone knows," Pablo said. "Someone does know."

"Should we start painting?" Connor asked. He had brought his brush with him. Kara glared at him. "Sorry. I didn't mean it."

"Who could paint at a time like this?" Pablo asked.

"It's a time to ponder, not to paint," Nigel said. "You know, you two kids. My cousin Rocco is having a Junk show tonight. Connor knows the place. I was on the phone with him this morning, and he's completely fine, which is a miracle, mind you. The left side of his house has blown clean off. The right side, it is all good. That's where he lives. The other side, that fellow did not fare very well, I am sorry to say. But what he loved most was that basement, and the music they played there. So they want to throw him a real party, in his memory. He was a friend of the band, as they say."

"That's messed up," Kara said. "Don't you think?"

"Yes. But it's Rocco's job to sort it. If he thinks this is what his friend wants, that is what he should do. Anyways, you two should go. I can't go, I have to mind the guest room for Pablo."

"Friend of the band—I like that," Pablo said. "I've always wanted to be a friend of the band. Any band would do. Friend of the band Yes, that sounds good. If I go poof one day, they'll throw a concert for me. A great way to go."

"I can't decide if that's insensitive or not," Kara said. "But I'll tell you what. If I ever start a band, you can be its friend."

"Really?"

She laughed. "Maybe we're a band already."

6

He noticed Kara laughing. He would always try to look at her when she laughed. See how her laughter moved, how the room changed around it. They were on the way to the basement show, making each other laugh about nothing at all.

"There's no way you're gonna do that!" she said, stumbling forward.

"Oh I will," Connor replied. "Hey cousin! It's me! You know me man, it's Connor, we go way back." he turned to her. "And my friend here really wants to meet you! She's your biggest fan."

"I'm sure that will work," Kara laughed. "Still though, when Nigel said his cousin was in a band, he didn't say it was Sherlock Holmes and the Panty Sniffers!"

Led by their frontman, Sherlock Holmes, the Panty Sniffers were considered one of the most funky junk bands around, one of a few that broke out of the local scene and gained mainstream appeal. It was a treat to see them back in their hometown, on one of their visits. They tried to pay homage to their roots with these shows, only letting the locals know what was about to happen. Still, word had spread, and it was going to be a busy night at the Kingdom of Joy.

The venue was on the verge of falling over. The vinyl-sided duplex had been cloven in two, with the shared wall blackened, but still standing. A man in black stood in front of the door, which opened to a vestibule once shared by both apartments and a staircase to the basement below, all of which was now plainly visible from the street. After taking five dollars each from Connor and Kara, the bouncer picked up the door (which no longer had hinges to attach to) and held it aside to let them enter.

"Is this like, structurally sound?" Kara asked.

"If it was safe, it wouldn't be Junk," he replied.

They headed downstairs to the venue. The room was cramped, the ceiling not far above Connor's head, with little ventilation to speak of. The band didn't have a stage, more just a corner of the room that they were setting up in. Kara and Connor found themselves being bumped and shuffled by the mass of people flowing into the room to the opposite corner. And in the middle of the room—a structural beam, a water heater, and several pipes, blocking their view.

"You know, this is probably better anyway," Kara said. She was pressed up against him. "These guys can get pretty loud."

Somehow Connor doubted that a pole would be of much assistance in blocking the sound. The bassist played a tuning note on his guitar. The blast from the speaker shook the damaged foundations of the building, sending a small cloud of dust from the ceiling. A silence fell on the room.

"We're gonna tear this place down!" the singer shouted into the mic. The room erupted in cheers.

"That was so cool," Kara said. "It's like they planned it. Anyway, see those guys up front?"

There were some people about their age lined up inches from where the band had set up. Even though there wasn't even any music on, they were nodding their heads and starting to dance. They all had beers in their hands, and a couple were even vaping. Connor always thought that it was cool to vape, but he didn't want to do it personally. It always seemed like it would be hard to keep up with, and cost money he didn't have.

"They look like they could be a bit better dressed," he said.

Kara laughed. "They thrift. I thrift too. I'm just better at it."

"If that's what you call it," he replied.

"Okay, anyway. This band is definitely one of my favorites. I know you're probably sick of hearing about them, being a local guy and all--"

Wow, she thought he was a local guy. That was awesome. He was someone you'd see around town. She grabbed his elbow and leaned closer. Connor reasoned that it was loud in the room already, so she needed to get closer. There was nothing weird about that. "—but this part is actually really interesting. Sherlock, you know, the singer guy, he is like, super specific about how the show is supposed to go. He doesn't want to be seen making any signals to the band or talking to them, he thinks it's unprofessional. They always play 'Fruit Feeler' first, but the first thirty seconds of that song is improvised—you know, it's chaos, they're all playing whatever. It has its roots in free jazz. So you ask yourself—" She was shouting now, to be heard over the mass of people in the room. "—how does the band know when to come in? Well, that's just it. I don't think they even know."

As Connor opened his mouth to reply, the band began to play, all at once, guitars and drums arguing, not making much music at all. He thought he heard a saxophone from behind the pole, something he found surprising – saxes were always tacky in a rock setting, but Junk bands were always experimenting with obscure instruments like that. Gradually, the band eased the noise, fell into a groove, and Holmes began to sing.

I love the produce aisle, I love to touch the fruit.
Fruit's the thing for me, beans just make me toot.
Bananas, apples, pears and limes!
I want to eat them all the time!
And you may wonder here, you may want to see
Me walking here, touching fruit in all this glee
He used to do normal things, didn't he?
Well, I'm stuck with the life you gave me!

The verse was more than a bit catchy, despite the offbeat lyrics. There were no other verses, and by the third time they played it, he found himself singing along with the rest of the audience. The song finished to a loud cheer from the audience, pleased to see a famous band up close. Kara seemed to truly feel like herself at the show, dancing along to each song, talking over the crowd during the breaks to give him her thoughts about them.

The band took a break after about an hour, and they escaped up a different set of basement stairs to a grassy backyard. Connor sat beside Kara on a short wall, enjoying the fresh air. He coughed and thought he saw dust escape from his mouth. Stumbling out of the basement was a bald man, with a Soviet hockey jersey. He leaned over to Kara, one hand on his knee as he caught his breath, and held out an already-lit joint. "A hit," he said, in a thick accent, looking up at her, his eyes red. "Is good for you."

"Thanks, but I don't smoke anymore," she said, rolling her eyes as she looked back at Connor. "Bad for your lungs."

The man laughed. "Someone told me, you only go around once," he said. "Maybe next time you go around, you have some weed."

"You know, I'd take a hit," Connor said, wanting to be cool.

"Sorry," the man replied, taking a drag on his own. "You are a skinny boy, you stick to vaping. This is just between me and the beautiful woman." What was he on about? It was cool to vape.

The cloud of weed smoke rising from the backyard had begun to block out the stars. Connor craned his neck to watch it happen. "What you looking at?" Kara asked. "Counting stars?"

There was too much light in the city for there to be stars. "Counting the dark," he said.

"That's the stupidest, most dramatic thing you've ever said," she laughed. "Did you take a hit while I wasn't looking?"

Well, that was an extreme reaction, he thought. He made a mental note not to try and say fake deep stuff in the future.

"Oh, I'm sorry I said that," she said. "Sometimes I just say stuff. Let's go back inside, I don't want to miss the set." Then, something peculiar happened. As she kept on with her apology, she leaned over and kissed him, practically mid-sentence. She grabbed his arm and stood him up. "I want to see if there's a spot we can see better. Let's go."

He let himself be guided back down into the damp and dusty basement of the half-building. He took a deep breath, trying to quell the sickness in his stomach. Maybe he'd think about it later. She certainly didn't seem to be thinking about it very much—he watched her intently watch the action on stage as it started again. He remembered the advice a friend gave him once: When you're nervous, just have two or three sips of beer. He spotted the dude with the hockey jersey lording over some girl, one who seemed much more receptive to his charms. There was a beer can sticking out of the back pocket of his jeans. Connor walked over and slipped the beer can out of his pocket. He walked back over to Kara as he sipped it, finding it warm and unappetizing. He crushed the can in his fist and stuffed it into his pocket. He did not feel any less nervous but felt cool for taking something off the guy. He was sure that the man was really missing the two or three sips of beer he'd stolen from him by now.

The rest of the show was fine. Connor floated along with the music; he wasn't very familiar with the band, though he'd heard of it. It was made better by Kara. She knew all the songs, mouthing along to the chorus, nodding along as vigorously as the well-dressed fans up at the front, raising her arms at times when the vibe called for it. As the show wrapped up and the singer dismissed the crowd, he convinced her to make an introduction to the lead singer.

"Sherlock!" she exclaimed. "I'm Kara." She reached to shake his hand, and he accepted it.

"Uh, nice to meet you," he smiled. He was tall and bald, with patchy stubble and a mustache. Every girl in town loved his mustache.

"I just loved the show," she said. "But I have to ask—and I know you must get this all the time—how does the band know when to come in? You know, after the free part in the first song?"

He rubbed his chin. "Yeah you know... it's actually the same length each time. Yeah, I made Bobby and Joey learn to count to 28 while playing. We have one of those analog clocks in the place where we practice. I would make one of us sit out and count out loud while looking at the clock. Just shouting one, two, three over the music. It wasn't so bad. You can learn anything that way." He turned away to fiddle with his guitar case, indicating he had no further interest in the conversation.

That night, Kara sat in her bed and opened a book. Connor laid in his own bed. There was a lot he probably could have said to her then. He thought of what they'd shared earlier, and it worried him, though he wasn't sure why yet. When he looked over at her, he felt warmer about it. She lowered her book to her lap.

"That guy was just the coolest. I had no idea that they always played the group solo for 28 seconds." She grinned at him.

"Kara," he said, rolling away from her. "I think he was fucking with you."

7

Pablo held a portion of the rope barrier above his head to let the others in. Various roads, paths, and sections of forest had been roped off where the construction (or deconstruction) work was ongoing. Just after the boundary, the forest had the same look it always did, pinecones on the ground, pine trees in the sky, birds chirping, and the wind. It was only a few hours after dawn. Walking in the forest usually meant a small cloak of darkness, as the tree canopy closed overhead; but as they walked, the forest got brighter, and the group could see between the pines. The trees stopped at a small stream. The other side had trees, but they were felled, stripped of branches, or turned to dust. The soil had an ashen quality to it, as it still had not rained. A snow-white rabbit hopped along in the charcoal dust, unaware, its feet stained gray.

"Oh, it's a baby," Nigel noted.

"The domestic rabbit–a most gruesome capitalist invention," Pablo said, crossing the stream and trying to approach the rabbit. It just hopped away, as rabbits do when faced with strangers.

And so they walked along the stream, forest on one side, the wasteland on the other, without speaking much. Connor reckoned that the destruction reached for almost a mile. Many buildings that seemed to be damaged and in the process of collapsing, furniture and insulation spilling out. The strangest thing was how open it all was—you never used to be able to see this far, at this angle. It was only at a few vantage points that you could see the maze of the neighborhood, and even then your view was blocked by many buildings. Now there was nothing to block one's view.

Past the crest of the next hill was a small concrete structure, cracked and collapsed, a pile of rubble half-standing up. The rebar was sticking out of the walls, twisted and bent where chunks had fallen out of the building. It seemed impossible that metal could bend like that. As they got closer, Pablo began running up the hill. "My god," he said. "It's the radio tower!"

A large radio tower had bent and broken like a tree in a storm and lay smashed on the ground further downstream. Satellite dishes lay strewn about. Connor realized it was the broadcasting station for WJNK, the local radio station. He wasn't a big fan of radio, but he felt a small pain in his chest. Those were local guys who ran the station, they did a good job and they gave all the local bands a fair shot. He couldn't imagine how expensive it might be to rebuild the tower.

As they rounded the back of the building, they saw a man in a hard hat and reflective vest sitting on the ground, leaning against the building. He looked out at the broken tower and at the wasteland beyond.

"Yo," Connor said. "Tommy? That you?"

He'd known Tommy since high school. He always felt weird about him—it wasn't who Tommy was that was the problem—it was what he did. "Yeah, man. How's it been?"

He dapped Connor up, without standing. His face seemed dirty, but Connor wasn't sure if it was the shadow of a beard he was wearing or dust.

"Good, man. You know, the usual. Kind of a situation over here, right?"

"Yeah, dude. Tell me about it," he said, wiping his brow. "My dad has me working overtime this week."

"Doesn't your dad own an explosives company?" Connor asked. It was the inevitable question. Tommy did work for an explosives company, just like his father and his grandfather before him. The other people in the group went silent at the comment.

"Yeah dude. They just called us in. Everything is, like, contaminated. All those buildings and shit—we're just leveling them. So then they just take a bulldozer in and sweep it all into a truck and be done."

Connor thought of the show he'd been to and the half-broken house. That would probably have to be blown up as well, His apartment, too. The soot on the walls, the chemicals in the air. "But why are you over here?"

"There's this word I learned. I think it's Japanese in origin. I read it in a book—me in a book, can you believe it? Ennui. It means you're sad about the way your life turned out. So I walked over here. Well, you know, I'm actually on my lunch break, I'll be back at it soon. But I like to imagine that I just could walk away from it all, sit on a hill and be sad about it."

"I'm sorry, Tommy," Connor said. "I don't know how to help you."

"Well, you know how to rig explosives?" he laughed. "I'll be okay. I should really be off. Stay safe guys." He slowly stood to his feet and shambled off.

"Bomb technician. Seems like a jolly fellow," Nigel said. "Should we follow him?"

"Aren't there bombs over there?" Stirbert said. "Like, actual bombs? That blow things up?"

"I mean, he's still in one piece," Nigel said, starting to walk. "And haven't you ever wanted to see something explode?"

"For some reason, I remember seeing something explode very recently," Kara said

"I'm with her," Connor said. "But still, maybe we'll figure something out. Find someone who knows what the heck happened." The group agreed to go on. By then, there had been news that there was some sort of chemical accident related to the train derailment, but there wasn't much else known. They were eager to investigate.

Connor tried to walk beside Kara. They both had fun last night, and she'd said as much on their walk back, but it remained that nothing happened. She wasn't her usual talkative self. He reasoned with himself that he'd be satisfied holding her hand. They didn't need to kiss again if she didn't want to. Not again. But if he could touch her hand, maybe it would feel real.

"Last night," he said, regretting speaking. "You were sober?"

"Yeah," she smiled. "Why do you ask?"

He shook his head. "No, no reason at all." And there was nothing else to say.

The five travelers wound their way down the hill, following a path beside the stream. A flock of seagulls had flown in to inspect the damage, pecking at chunks of black dirt and burnt plants. In the distance several dump trucks were lined up, taking loads of debris one by one. There was even a crane pecking at a pile of concrete, in its own slow manner. As they walked, the sky grew paler and turned a shade of steel that again dulled to gray as the clouds filled with fluid.

He watched her. She had a habit of rocking side to side as she walked along, nodding her head to one side or the other. She seemed to have a fascination with her left hand; she was always rubbing her thumb across the pads of her other fingers, or spreading them out as far as she could. She had a blue plastic ring on her middle finger with a bird's face on it. She'd shown it to him once. "I'm not much for jewelry," she had explained, "but this little guy was hard to pass up." She had a way of making him feel like a loser—not with something she said, did, or even meant, just in the way she could be desirable, the way she could command his attention, the way she could affect something external on the world of man without trying. It made him jealous. The older he got, the more he started thinking that nothing he did mattered much at all. She seemed to matter a lot. Thinking about her—about what they were—stressed him out, but looking at her: that didn't hurt at all.

The path led them to the edge of the work site. Construction workers sorting bricks into one pile, metal into another, working on an endless pile of scrap. Nigel led the group around the corner of one half-standing building to get a better look. A man with a reflective vest over his polo shirt walked around the corner. "Hey kids," he said, smiling genuinely. "It's not safe. Get outta here."

"Sure thing, sir," Nigel said. "But I have a query for you, if you don't mind. Is it safe here? Should we be 'getting out of town', as it were?"

"Well, I'm what you might call a subcontractor," the man said. He seemed happy to answer a question. "I work for a company that recycles masonry, bricks and all that. We just come and take the bricks. We're not the EPA or anyone like that. But—you might want to ask those people over there." He pointed his clipboard at a roped off area with two dozen people standing behind it. Nigel and the others could be forgiven for not noticing them—despite holding signs of protest with slogans, flags, and the like, they were not shouting anything. They seemed to be chatting amongst themselves. Several of them wore gas masks.

Nigel always dug stuff like this. He happily trotted to the edge of the restricted area and ducked under the rope. Connor followed as he approached a middle-aged man holding a sign: EPA: HANDS OFF OUR KIDS it read. "Hello sir," Nigel said. "What could be the matter?"

"Ah a Brit, is that right?" he spat. "I'm not sure if what I'm upset about even would make sense to you. Brits don't have rights at all! They just read tabloids and watch their 'telly' and that's all they know! In this free country, we have our sacred right to protest."

"Right-o, sir," Nigel said, straightening. "Perhaps you could simplify it, for someone of my low character."

The man agreed. "Yeah. Well you see, those stupid idiots. Hey, stupid idiots! Go home!" He shook his fist at the construction workers. "Our little town was perfect the way it was. I still remember when I moved here ten years ago. You know, none of this overdevelopment nonsense. You could drive anywhere you wanted. You could even drive to the pharmacy, and it wouldn't take you more than ten minutes, and you could park anywhere you wanted. You could park on the sidewalk. You know, they don't like it when a group of people is so happy and has everything they need, so they fill the place with chemicals to ruin it. Yes sir, I don't believe that gobbledygook about the skateboard on the tracks for one second. They blew up that train on purpose. Now they want to build apartments on the chemicals. No, I won't stand for that. It's up to us, regular people, to clean house around here, just like we did when the Brits were in town, no offense to you by the way. There's more of us than there are of them!" He paused as he ran out of breath.

"Well, aren't they cleaning it up?" Nigel asked, amused by the speech. "I don't think they can build apartments if it wasn't all cleaned up. Besides, there were apartments there before."

"Well, you haven't been here," the man replied. "I've been on the ground. I've been doing the work. And what you see here is land clearance. The chemicals are in the water. Yes, they're in the water. The soil, I could care less, but the water is what matters. But he might not want to, because you're stupid. Anyway, these chemicals are drivers of forced feminization. They want to turn our beautiful, strong boys into girls, and our girls, well, into super-girls. It's just not natural. Of course, any forced feminization should be done with consent at the forefront, as I always say. I don't care what you do in your bedroom, but leave me and my family out of it. But what happens when these new apartments are sold to unsuspecting, hard-working people, who then unknowingly consume these disastrous chemicals? Only the total breakdown of Western society! I could weep. I trace my lineage back to the emperors of Rome, you know – when Charlemagne had his head split by an axe, and an angel came down from heaven to push the two halves of his head back together so he could save Christian society, I still feel that pain. That's generational trauma."

"Wait–what happened to Charlemagne?" Connor asked.

"It's not my job to educate you," the man replied. "Either you know your history, or you don't. Looking at you, it looks like you don't know the first thing about Charlemagne."

Nigel shook the man's hand. "Well, thank you, sir. It's been a pleasure. You've certainly given me a lot to think about."

Pablo laughed as they walked away. "At home, that's what we call an expert on Frankish rulers."

"I'm not sure what that means–is that a metaphor?" Nigel asked. "That sounds like, literally what he is. Well, I can't speak to the historical aspects of it. I think he may have been exaggerating about the axe, but certainly he's a big fan of the old governor Charlemagne, that sorry fellow. Connor, don't listen to Pablo, he's gone out over his skis on this one. See, a real metaphor! Not something I made up!"

Their bickering was amusing to the rest of the group, but Connor was still basking in the glow of their conversation with the protester. It was amazing to just hear someone spew something interesting and stupid, even if it had undertones of something awful. Nigel's British accent had a talent for drawing those kinds of people out.

There was a scuffle behind them, with two men shouting. Connor turned, and nobody other than Stirbert was trading blows with the protester they'd just made conversation with! "Hey man, get back!" Nigel shouted, running over to grab him. Kara tried to lay hands on the burly protester but was shaken off. Nigel pulled Stirbert off, whose nose was covered in a moderate amount of blood. His glasses had been thrown to the floor.

"Heathen! Demon!" the protester said, pointing at Stirbert, allowing Pablo to hold him back. "Nonce!" he said, nodding to Nigel, hoping for approval of his Britishism. "I won't let you get away with this!"

"Oh shut up, you stupid psycho!" Stirbert said. "Do your kids talk to you? Do you know you have grandkids? No, Daddy's protesting something he read on the fucking internet!"

Everyone was agape. Connor wasn't sure he'd ever heard Stirbert say that many words in a row, much less that amount of bile. "What happened, man?" Nigel asked.

"He said—he said something about—" Stirbert stammered.

"Alright man, let's calm down. Let's worry about this later. We gotta get you cleaned up." Pablo dabbed at his face with his shirt, but Stirbert swatted him off, still hot.

"Oh, he's bleeding," Kara said, turning away. "That's so gross. I can't deal with that. What the heck." As if she was the one that just got beat up. He felt a little sick. They all liked to beat up on Stirbert a little, he was an odd little guy—but never physically. Plus, he was part of the team. That just wasn't right. Nigel and Pablo mumbled reassurances to Stirbert, who looked a little worse for wear. Connor reasoned that he was probably just shaken up.

"Do we tell his dad?" Connor said.

"No, I don't think he'd like that," Pablo said. "Plus, where's dad now? I don't see him. Too bad for him that he's not here and his son is getting taken care of by poor old Pablo."

Nigel's house, which was luckily still standing, was not too far of a walk down the road, and the two of them took him inside. Nigel's apartment was a little cramped, so Kara and Connor stayed outside, and the group agreed to split up. Connor gave Stirbert his best wishes, who was not one for talking at the moment. The clouds continued to grow from the horizon to over their heads, cloaking the city in a shade of gray, but the rain wouldn't come.

And the two of them walked through the city, not speaking. Since they'd started living together, there'd been a lot of talking. What the weather was, what Pablo and Nigel were getting up to, what was going to happen to the town, what music they liked to listen to. Her loquaciousness fit in well with the group. Now, they were past that point. Connor still wondered what she thought of him. Their room had two twin beds on either side of the room. In the evening, they'd chat for a bit before going to sleep, and that would be that. And he figured he was okay with that, despite how he felt about her. He wasn't sure where he'd go if things went sour between them—maybe he'd have to sleep on Nigel's couch.

"Do you know the way?" she asked. "I don't recognize this street."

He told her he knew the way. She could have some weird habits. She liked to have ibuprofen (just one) with her lunch most days, because of her 'bad knees'. He was pretty sure she was 23, but she wouldn't tell him her birthday—she refused whenever he asked. She had friends that lived in her old town, and she'd walk to see them, and the walk was probably an hour, she'd said. He knew nothing about them though, or what they were like, or their names. She had a habit of being incredibly vague about things – 'we went to the store' or 'we got Chinese food' was usually all he could get out of her.

"Would you want to see a movie later?" she asked.

"Yeah," Connor said. "I got nothing going on. You can pick." She could be a little mean for no reason. She always said it was her tongue moving quicker than her brain, but he always thought she could try a little harder to be nicer. Just do a little more thinking. He wondered if that was just how someone as confident as her usually acted. He had started to like that about her. It was bad to filter too much of your personality through social expectations.

"Well, this is it," Connor said as they rounded the corner. He stopped and leaned against the vinyl siding of the hotel, looking at her. She stopped as well and folded her arms. What a silly way to look at someone, he thought. What a silly life he lived.

"I feel like I can't get a word out of you today," she said, smiling. She tapped her right foot on the concrete.

"I feel like twenty different things happened," he said. She didn't say anything back but continued smiling. She tapped her foot again. "What," he said. "Now you're not gonna say anything?"

She took a step towards him and looked into his eyes. "This part is always awkward," she said. She grabbed his shirt with both hands and kissed him. He reached both his hands around her back to pull her closer, and she let him.

8

Vincent Reznor found himself laid up in a hospital bed, and nothing hurt at all. He looked out at his legs, covered by a bed sheet, and tried to wiggle his toes, and they seemed to move. Alright, we still got toes, that's electric, he thought. His eyes continued to adjust to the fluorescent lights. Where the hell was his vape? A hit would be insane right now. Just the thought of it brought blood flowing back into his limbs. An IV had been stuck into his left arm. What the hell had gone down?

A doctor came strolling into the room, wearing a white coat, a clipboard in his hand. Vincent thought he looked like an old fart–someone who would try to take your vape if he could. "Yo," he said to the doctor. "Doc, what's going on?"

The doctor wrote something in his chart. "Interesting," he said. "So you don't know?"

"Nah, man," Vincent replied. He tried to think. "I was at work, you know. I was cooking. I think I clocked out, and now I wake up here. Makes no sense. Am I hurt?"

"Well, man," the doctor said, mocking him, "—as far as we know, you were out on your skateboard near the railroad tracks on Fulkerson Street. There was a chemical accident due to a train derailment–are you sure you haven't heard about this?"

"What do you mean, man!" Vincent fumed. "I just woke up, bro!"

The crash of metal against metal. A column of fire into the sky. Smoke of three different colors. Ash in his hair, in his face. His board, buried in the rubble.

"Yeah, but I threw the TV on, thought maybe you'd get the gist of it while you were asleep. Anyways—you were very close to the epicenter of the spill. We think you breathed in some kind of neurotoxin, some combination of chemicals the train was carrying... and it knocked you out for a few days. But, you're awake now, so it seems to be improving."

"Dude, that's it man?" Vincent asked. "Like, you gotta get that stuff out of my brain man. I could go crazy. What if I start biting people or some shit? What if I become a zombie?"

"As your doctor, I would advise you not to bite people."

"Nah, but the neuro– the neurotoxin, it could mess me up really good."

"Just don't bite anyone. You're going to be fine," the doctor said. "Promise me you won't bite anyone.'

"Yessir," Vincent said. "No bites from this guy."

"Anyways, you have someone you owe a lot of thanks, besides me of course. Do you know this girl?" he stepped to the side. Asleep on a chair was Mack, the girl from the record store. She had not woken up during their conversation, and her tongue was just poking out of her mouth. She always slept like an idiot.

"Yo, Mack!" he shouted. "Yo! You're here, man!" She grumbled something, starting to wake up.

The doctor checked his chart. "Your girlfriend here was, according to her, 'smoking weed behind the store'. She happened to hear the explosion, and when she went to see what was happening, saw you. Somehow she carried you two miles to the hospital on her back. It seems to have taken a lot out of her. She's been sleeping here, bothering the nurses."

"Damn baby, how'd you do that?" Vincent said.

She was awake now. She leaped from the chair, and hopped up on the bed, straddling him. She shook her head a bit and pushed her hair behind her ears. She looked like she could still fall asleep. Out of her pocket, she pulled his vape. His vape! She saved the vape! She took a long drag, her eyelids fluttering as she did so—and immediately plunged down, planting the smoke into his lungs with a kiss.

"RAH!!!!!" Vincent shouted, immediately sitting up in bed. The action threw Mack off of him. "Yo, doc, I'm better now! Get me outta here!" he said.

"No, we're not doing this," the doctor said. "Security! Security!"

Mack pushed him back down onto the bed. "You're mine, you stupid piece of shit," she said. "I saved your dog ass. Don't forget that. Stacy didn't save you, Julie didn't, Bertha didn't. You're not gonna talk to those girls anymore."

"Fine, bro," Vincent said. "I won't."

9

Connor and Kara sat across the table from one another at the coffee shop. It was nearly lunchtime, but a long night and late morning had delayed the start of their day. The seating in the coffee shop was limited. The tables were placed against the windows—one person sat in a chair and another on the windowsill. The cool glass against Connor's shirt felt strange against the heat from the hot water fin tube radiator against his legs. A bookshelf sat on the opposite wall from him, filled with books he'd never seen anyone reading, and besides that many photos of muscle men from a century ago. A pair of boxing gloves hung in the corner.

"A latte for you, and an iced tea for the lady," the worker said, placing two cups in front of them. The worker was none other than Steve Balboni, an old friend of his. He stood smiling at them, waiting for Connor to strike up a conversation.

"Thanks, Steve Balboni," Connor said. "We can pay, really. You don't have to do this."

"Well, it costs the shop about fifty cents in beans to make coffee. And there's the rent of the coffee shop, going by the listing online, assuming they pay market rate, they pay about ten cents per cup of coffee to the landlord. I am worth about thirty cents of that cup of coffee, given how slow business has been today. Two drinks, call that two dollars, just about. The cost of that order you just made would probably be about fourteen dollars after tax. And I gave it to you for free, because you're my friend. So if you can, try to enjoy the drinks an amount equal to two dollars. If you tried to enjoy them for the full price, you'd leave disappointed. I am never supposed to disappoint customers. In a way, I'm saving the shop money.

Steve Balboni walked away with that. "Steve Balboni. What a nice dude," Kara said. "What'd you do to make him like you so much?"

"Nothing specific," he said. "He seemed like a nice enough guy, so I came around a lot to the shop. Asked him his thoughts on life, and what he was doing. Then one day he decided I was cool, too. You'd think he owns the place, how he treats it. Every surface in here, he finds a way to clean it. One time I caught him washing the underside of all the tables—apparently some teenager had been sticking gum to one of them for years. He couldn't stand it. I think he banned the kid from ever coming back."

"That's sweet," Kara replied. She looked frazzled—in a good way. A few things about her were out of place. "Can we talk ground rules?"

"I don't know what you mean."

She reached her hand across the table to take his hand. "Like this. First, I don't want to tell the guys we're in a relationship."

"Okay."

"I just mean that I don't want to be, like, official yet," Kara said. "Nothing wrong with what's going on, but you can't just go screaming it from the rooftops. We can do that soon. But mentally, you know, I have to take one step at a time. This is my first step."

"I guess that makes sense," he said. He played with her fingers in his hand, squeezing one of them, looking at it.

"Second, and I guess I said this already, but don't tell Pablo."

"I mean, why? He's my boy. I have to tell them if something like this happens."

"For me," she said. "I just don't want to change their perception of me. I have to figure it out in my own head before I can have everyone know everything. Why it happened, what it means. Just do it for me."

"Okay," he said. She pulled her hand away and sipped her tea.

"So, what do you think happened?" Connor asked, trying to find a new subject. "Out there."

"I mean, I think it happened exactly like they're saying," she said. "Train crashes, fire rains from the sky. I mean, what else? Seems simple-ish."

"I know, but how are people getting from that to all these conspiracies about the chemicals?"

"They might just need someone to blame."

"I mean, maybe. But there probably is someone to blame. Like in a literal sense. It didn't do that for no reason. I mean, I guess 'no reason' is a valid reason. But usually they look into it, and they find out someone made a huge mistake. I imagine that person feels pretty bad right now."

"It's a pretty big mistake to make. A world-historical mistake," she said. "Did you see there's a Wikipedia article for it now?"

"Yeah, I did." He didn't feel like telling her that Steve Balboni wrote most of it, and bragged about it to Connor. He also didn't want to say that Connor had snapped a photo of the wreckage, for Steve Balboni to add to the article. He also didn't want to tell her that it was pretty easy to write an article on Wikipedia, since it was the free encyclopedia that anyone can edit. Even guys like Steve Balboni.

"Hey, Steve Balboni," Connor said, looking over at him. Nobody was in the shop besides Connor, Kara, and Steve Balboni, and in moments like that Steve Balboni would find time to edit on his laptop. He sat on a stool behind the counter, hunched over the computer, his hair falling in his eyes. He typed furiously for a moment, clicked once, and then closed the laptop.

"Sorry guys," Steve Balboni said. "Dealing with this vandal. Someone keeps adding cartoon characters to the death toll from the train derailment. I'm trying to stop him, but it's slow going. Anyway, I shouldn't say all that, not to you guys. If someone is drawing attention to themselves on Wikipedia, we as editors are asked to deny them further attention. How can I be of service to you?" He clasped his hands together and smiled.

"We were just wondering if you had any inside info about that whole train thing," Connor asked. "We're just kind of in the dark about it."

Steve Balboni brightened at the question. "Well, here's what I know—every week for the last thirty years, a locomotive rolls through here on her way to a manufacturing facility in rural Connecticut. Unfortunately, I don't know what was on the train. The shipment was for a defense contractor, so it's classified. I can't say exactly. As for why the train derailed at all—well, the first thing you should know is that trains are very safe. They get in accidents less often than semi trucks do, and that makes them a great choice for delivering dangerous materials."

"Sometimes there's an issue with the track, and for whatever reason, the train is traveling above the safe speed for that track. When that happens, the train can derail. We're not so sure if that happened here. The fire actually burned so hot that it melted most of the cars closest to the explosion, and, well, you know that much of the neighborhood has been badly damaged. Those are things that seem impossible to me, but I'm no expert on that subject. The authorities have been gathering what little CCTV footage exists, but nothing's been released to the public."

None of that was incredibly new information to him. People had been talking about it—on the street, before bed, on the internet. Nobody seemed to have a definitive answer, besides those whose theories were too outlandish to believe. Connor understood those people, too. Things did seem unbelievable. They could have it exactly right.

"Did you catch the protest?" Kara asked. "Over by the pile."

Steve Balboni frowned. "I did. My uncle actually was with them. He got bored and went home. His wife called and asked him where he was, but he didn't have a good answer. Funny, stuff like that. But yeah, any kind of chemical stuff, he is on that like a moth to a flame. He's always opposing various chemicals."

"That sounds stimulating for him," Connor said.

"It's not him I'm worried about," Steve Balboni said. "Guys like him, it's a hobby. They know in the back of their minds that it doesn't matter. Bad shit happens, blame someone, protest it. Fits in the framework of whatever the real thing is they've been mad about their whole lives, and it's more proof that they were right all along... it's my aunt I'm worried about."

"What's your aunt do again?" Connor asked.

Steve Balboni leaned against the table, glancing at the open door to the shop. The table started to tip, and Kara had to lunge to keep her drink steady. "She's a city councilor," he said.

"Why's that matter?"

"Well, I mean, Connor, you got kicked out of your apartment, right?"

"Yeah, I did. Kara did too."

"Where are you gonna go when that hotel stay is up?"

"Shoot, I don't know," Connor said. He hadn't really gotten that far. "I guessed I would have my apartment back. They just had to clean it."

"Dude," Steve Balboni said. He paused. "They're knocking the whole thing down."

"What?"

"They're knocking it down." He made a sweeping motion with his hand. "It's contaminated. Or something like that."

"I guess that makes sense." He did not think that it made sense. He wasn't sure why he said that, really.

"It's not just you, either. There's like, two, three thousand people who are with friends, in hotels, sleeping in the high school gymnasium, whatever. And you'd think, maybe they'd clean it up, repair what they could, put up some new buildings, and everyone could go home and pick up where they left off. But that's the thing—my aunt and uncle are married for a reason. They get along. And my aunt doesn't want that to happen, at all."

"Because of the chemicals?"

"The chemicals, maybe. But they'll have that cleaned up eventually. I mean, if you believe them, I guess. But a lot of money is being spent to clean it up, so it had better be. I asked her about it. She just doesn't want them to build anything at all."

"What's that mean?" Kara asked. "Nothing at all?"

"She says it was too crowded and noisy in the city. That people were up to no good over there. And I, uh, obviously don't agree with all that. I know that's your neighborhood. You'll have to ask her if you want the full story, I try not to listen to her too much. But that's what's happening. From what she said, things were moving pretty fast. They hired this famous architect already."

"That's so fucked!" Kara exclaimed. "That's where we live!"

"I don't understand," Connor said. The world started to close in on him, and he couldn't speak.

"What's nothing? What good is nothing?" she continued. "This place is already kind of nowhere. Why make it less than that? It's our place. It's where my apartment is, and my plants, and my clothes. I want all that stuff back. I'd like my home back. What's her problem with me?"

"Listen," Steve Balboni replied. He glanced over his shoulder again. A customer was politely waiting to order a coffee. His face was flushed. "I have to go now. I have to help this customer. I'm sorry, I'm so sorry. I was never close to her. Please don't be mad at me. We can hang out later, if you like. I'll make you dinner. Oh, but I only have croissants at the house. Dang it. Maybe I'll pick up a pizza. Are you a vegetarian, ma'am? Sorry—I have to go."

He scuttled behind the counter and greeted the customer.

"Is he serious?" Kara asked, leaning forward.

"Yo, it's not his fault," Connor said. "And I know him. He couldn't tell a lie if he wanted to."

"What are we gonna do? This is messed up shit."

"I don't know. I don't know. Maybe we can find out more. Talk to some people. See how serious this is."

"It seems pretty serious to me."

"People are serious all the time," Connor said. "Not everyone is serious about power."

"Is that Marx?"

"It's me."

"Good to know I'm living with a bad poet," she said, gathering her things. She stood up and started for the door.

"And sleeping with one," he said.

10

Nigel, Pablo, Kara, and Connor sat on a row of chairs in City Hall. Pablo and Nigel wore matching blue polos; where they'd found them, Connor had no idea. He suspected they were uniforms for a long-closed business. Connor wore a light green button-down with short sleeves. Kara had dug up a nicer pair of slacks for the occasion. The door next to them had a small placard that read: MAUREEN CRINGLESWORTH, CITY COUNCILOR. Connor fidgeted with his khakis, which didn't need a belt on account of them being too small for him. City Hall was a nice aging building, with faux marble columns in the hallways, lofty eleven-foot ceilings, and no air conditioning. Connor had set up a meeting with the councilor.

The door to the councilor's office swung open, and the protester they'd recently had a run-in with walked out. His face was beet red. He stopped in his tracks when he noticed the group. "I hope you're happy, I really hope you are," he said. "Chemicals! They are feeding our kids chemicals. And you're here to tell my wife how good of a job they are doing with those chemicals, I'm sure. Chemicals for breakfast, lunch, and dinner, that's you! If only you knew how bad things really were. She's not going to let you get away with it. That's all I'll say."

"Oh yeah," the man continued. "Is your little buddy okay? The one whose nose I smashed in?"

"Yeah, he's gonna be fine," Connor said. "Thanks."

"Yeah, it's just the marketplace of ideas," he said. He looked down at his clenched right fist and caressed it with his left hand. "It can get dangerous. That's how it goes in the free country we live in. Not everyone can handle it." He dusted off his overalls and trotted out of the building, having calmed down from the visit with the councilor.

A bell to the right of the door started ringing. It was a metal bell, no larger than a person's head, built into a square cutout in the wall of the hallway. The four of them sat and watched it. The longer they watched, the more it seemed to ring. "Come in!" a voice came from inside. "The bell means come! Read the sign!"

Sure enough, there was a sign by the bell saying 'The Bell Means Come'. How pleasant. At a large, wide wooden desk was a middle-aged woman with pale bleached blonde hair. She was holding a rope in her hand that ran across the room. She made a show of pulling it, causing the bell to ring. "See?" she said, her voice warm. "I don't have the budget for a secretary, so I have the bell. I don't like to raise my voice—or get up."

Pablo made a point of reaching over the desk and shaking her hand. "Wow, a firm handshake! You're a nice young man, aren't you?" she said, laughing.

Kara and Connor had already sat in the two available chairs, so Pablo and Nigel had to awkwardly back up and stand behind them. "Well, then," she asked. "What can I do for you?"

"Well, we all happen to be employees of a small painting company, and we have been out of work, thanks to the accident. Some of us also lost our homes. So as you can imagine, we are not in the most auspicious of situations. The temporary housing is only temporary, which is why we were hoping we'd be able to return to the neighborhood after it was rebuilt. But we heard from one of our friends, and then I think Connor grabbed a newspaper, and he saw something similar to what we heard—they're saying people don't want to have it rebuilt. And so we just wanted to ask you directly about it. I'm just struggling to understand what it all means, or why something like that would happen. And I think you can sympathize with the fact that we'd all like to go back to normal. I don't know where I'll go when the hotel stay ends. I might have to leave town. It's not like I can pick up a place at the back of the bay or the hill for what little hourly I get."

Councilor Cringlesworth plopped her Target-purchased flats up on the top of her broad-shouldered oak desk. The veins in her feet were blue and purple. She wove her fingers together behind her head and smiled grimly. "You know, it's a conundrum," she said. "I'm quite sympathetic. Growing up, I was one of five kids, and my dad wasn't around. My mom struggled to take care of us all. We had to move a lot—and you know, I think I learned a lot from that. It made me more resilient in the end. And that's all to say that as a city, we're tumbling along, we're stuttering, we're not adapting to the times. You know, I've been telling everyone that comes to this office, it's horrible that fire rained from the sky like it did. But if it wasn't the fire, it would have been something else. It wasn't sustainable. That neighborhood model, you know the whole dense, amenity-based thing, it's from a hundred, two hundred years ago. It's not safe anymore, it's not clean. It attracts crime, it attracts people from out-of-state. People there litter, they stay up late, they throw parties in the local park. I'm not saying you guys, specifically, are vagrants or criminals or what have you, of course not. Most people are law-abiding citizens. But maybe you're so used to it, that you have a higher tolerance for that sort of thing."

"And I think, I really think, that this is going to be the best for everyone. We're getting absurd amounts of funding from the federal government here, you know, and we can spend it on what we like. This is our opportunity to do something with that space. Imagine every nurse, every police officer, every firefighter gets their own parking space, in the heart of the city. Imagine a world-class urban park, designed by a renowned landscape architect. Suddenly this place is not kind of nowhere—we might be somewhere, after all. Somewhere that you're not always shaded in by tall buildings, mounds of trash. Somewhere you can find a parking spot, where you can go take in the birds and the sunshine if you want, have a picnic. Somewhere you can drive through safely and efficiently. That's all I want. And I wish, you know, that I could make more people see it. I can't just do everything for everyone, though. I'm elected to represent the interests of the whole city. I always want people to lean in, you know, listen to what I have to say, but I can't just let someone walk in here and change my mind. I'd be doing a disservice to those who elected me if I did."

"But that makes like, no sense, dude," Connor said. The paint on the walls of the office had been misapplied, and it looked wrong to his eye. "Real people live here. I think it's a fine neighborhood. Nobody was making you go there. I never had my stuff stolen and I didn't have problems with anybody. We all got along. You know, my life was great. It really was. I don't see how you know, in terms of a life improvement type of scenario, this helps me at all." Pablo was nodding along. He was usually the long-winded one, and probably liked to see Connor articulating himself.

"You're still in one piece, aren't you? Your friends are with you. You guys are going to walk out of here and do the same things you kids always did," the councilor said. She took her feet off the table and looked out the window. "I have to make trade-offs. Obviously, your life is worse in the short term, your house got blown up. Believe me, I am sympathetic to that. And you know, you can always come to my office if there's problems with the relief systems we've set up, or if you just need a shoulder to cry on. But long term, when you have some perspective, maybe a bit of distance from the situation, I hope you'll acknowledge that we had to make a difficult choice here, and we chose the thing that was best for the most people over the longest period of time."

Kara stood up, fuming. "Lady, that just sucks. There's so much we do over there you have no idea about. I mean, what's gonna happen to the music scene? You know how many bands have come out of there? The shows are–"

"Oh, the music," she interrupted, rolling her eyes. "The local college has practice rooms, I heard they're very soundproof. And I'll listen to a bit of Junk myself now and then, you know, my nephew loves the stuff. But neighbors have long complained about the noise. There's no reason for you guys to be having a blowout in a random basement each weekend. You live in a community–have some respect for it. Anyway, that's just my opinion on the matter. I apologize if that sounds rude."

Kara stood and made for the door. "Yeah, I'm outta here," she said. "And don't think I'll let you get away with this!"

Connor and the others thought it was as good a time as any to leave. "Thanks for your time," he said, and the councilor only smiled and nodded in response. They walked towards the lobby of the town hall. Connor felt sick again. He didn't know how someone could have things so backward and be so confident about it. He hated the polite way she insulted his friends, his community, and the powerlessness he felt over it. She was right, in a way–the thing she had wanted, for the neighborhood to be wiped off the face of the earth, had already happened.

As they approached the front entrance, a few workers had the doors held open for them by men in suits. They carried a large rectangular object covered by a sheet. They set it on a folding table in the center of the lobby. The four of them stood and looked at what was happening. "Oh, Maureen, my sweet jägerschnitzel! There you are!" one of them said in a thick German accent.

The councilor came striding out from behind the group and embraced the man. He kissed her on both cheeks. "Oh Vil, you're right on time!" she exclaimed. "And Helm, you haven't aged a day!" she went through the same sequence with the other well-dressed man.

"Is nice, my dear, to get out of the, how you say, Zoom box!" Vil said.

"Oh, how was your flight?" she asked. "Not too long I hope?"

"It is always long," he replied. "So very long. But worth it, to see your lovely face! And to show you my pretty things."

"And there comes Ben!" she said. A bald man of medium build and black-rimmed glasses stepped out from the other hallway. He wore a striped dress shirt with the first few buttons undone, and no tie. Connor knew him as the mayor of the city. In this town, the mayor was elected by a vote of the city council, not the people. Mayor Ben, as he liked to be called, shunned publicity and mostly worked directly with the council. That method seemed to help prevent him from attracting too much scrutiny. Some people joked that he probably didn't even live in town.

"Sirs," he said, extending a firm handshake. "It's great to finally meet you."

"Likewise," they both said.

"Shall we?" the mayor asked, extending his hand toward the covered object.

"Of course!" Helm said. He reached both his hands towards the sheet and wiggled his fingers above it for a moment. He wore several large silver rings. In one motion, he pulled the sheet off and tossed it to the floor.

"It's amazing!" the councilor said, clasping her hands together. The mayor said nothing, looking at it thoughtfully. Connor craned his neck to get a closer look. On the table was a diorama, complete with trees, clay models of people and cars, painted to the life. Connor found himself walking closer.

"Of course, there is first the matter of the memorial," Vil said, guiding the councilor's hand to the front of the display. Several obelisks, miniature versions of the Washington Monument, to honor this free country, each the height of a person who tragically lost their life. There is a reflecting pool; every day, the pool will glow green with built-in LED lights, to raise awareness for the environmental cleanup. The pool will also have a QR code in the bottom, for donations, uh, in lieu of throwing coins in the pool. That one is a code requirement. Silly Americans."

"Truly poignant," Cringlesworth said, putting her hand over her heart. She curled her bottom lip in a pout.

"And for the next part, we collaborated with the great American architect, P. Rudolph. We looked past his Yale credentials for this one because we needed the one thing he was truly expert in—parking lots. And this one is something that I think you'll find has you spitting out your Lager. Notice the native trees planted on the medians. Bioswales are provided for stormwater runoff. And of course," he pulled a miniature figure from the table. "There is you."

"It's wonderful!" Cringlesworth said. "My parking space!"

"And over here, the most splendid thing I can give to you. The grossvater of them all. The shining emerald on top of this city that you call nowhere. At several square kilometers, this will be one of the largest of its kind in the tri-state area. It is, uh, replete, with trails for walking, meadows for sitting, and in the middle is a pond with a respectful amount of geese and ducks. There is a new ball field for the humble baseballspieler of your local secondary school. And, if you look closely—" he plucked a miniature sign from the diorama and showed it to everyone in attendance. It showed a scooter crossed out with a red X. "Scooters, not allowable!"

"You thought of everything!" Cringlesworth said. "Scooters are such a nuisance." Connor was starting to find the presentation exhausting. Certainly, the whole diorama was well put together. And the park seemed like a nice park, on the whole—but the high school was probably a quarter mile down the road, and had a dozen fields of its own that were well-maintained. The forest (the portion of it that had not been destroyed, anyway) was not far from the other side of the tracks and had plenty of trails that were well-kept and safe. They'd just been out near those trails, painting the bridge, and they'd see joggers and people pushing babies in strollers, people enjoying the woods. How do you oppose a park? Stand against green space? The parking lot would be easy to knock, but it seemed like only a small portion of the land area, and people loved their parking. He was worried the plan would be quite popular. He knew this would upset Kara.

"Well, I could talk about this for hours, of course," Vil said, "but the last thing I have to show you is quite splendid. A smaller sheet, like the larger sheet that had covered the diorama, was covering a small shape on the edge of the park. "I present to you, the Government Services Center!" The building revealed was of brutalist concrete design, built in an upside down fashion, where the footprint of the building grew larger as it grew to its maximum of five floors. The thing seemed to be made of staircases – the building itself was like a set of steps, and you could walk up to any floor from any other floor by taking a wide, straight staircase. Black glass windows were set deep into the walls, to accentuate the implied strength of the building. Outside was a red brick plaza, flat and expansive, with a few tree plantings by the road. On the opposite side of the building was another small parking lot, surrounded by a chain-link fence.

"It's... tumescent," the mayor said. "I think this is the interaction with that state-level grant, yes?"

"Yes, indeed," Helm said. "This will be home to the Office of the Register of Deeds. It was originally going to be in a few floors of an office building in this neighborhood, but this was the perfect opportunity to make a statement. To build something that is a gift to the future of this city, and a memorial to what came before! What a joy it was to design something so fitting, so poignant. What a spectacular sight this will be. People will come from all over to marvel at this thing. They will clamor to work in this building, for the Register of Deeds. I could cry."

"When can we start?" the councilor asked.

11

Connor and Kara sat with each other in the hotel room, sharing a can of Boom. Her right leg was draped over his left. It was a lazy afternoon, and the temperature-controlled hotel room, complete with a perimeter induction unit, was an attractive place to be. The couch had a green corduroy finish. It was a replacement-level couch—an okay couch in the same way oranges were just an okay fruit.

"It's a one-hundred-year mistake," Connor said. "Some mistakes are ten-year mistakes. Like going bankrupt, or an expensive mattress. If you just wait ten years, you know, hang in there, it will be okay. This is something you probably can't fix for a hundred years, probably more."

"Yeah, I agree," she said, taking another sip. "I just don't know what we'd even do. I don't see myself stepping in front of a bulldozer."

"I'm not that brave either."

"Are we all doomed?"

"Not doomed. Nothing's really doomed, man. Things can be slightly worse or slightly better. Things are about to get worse. That isn't the end of the world. But too many bad things in a row, that's kind of a dangerous thing. You don't know what gets lost. One day, there's people out on the street, they get coffee, they ride bikes, they call taxis and all that, another day it's bad enough so they get up and leave. They just bring that energy somewhere else. And the place you had is not there. Just leaves blowing around in the wind, and asphalt."

"Okay, philosopher," she laughed. "And tell me about the building. What do you think of that?"

"It's like a spaceship landed on that place," Connor said. "I don't know what to make of it."

"I kind of like it," she said. "I mean, at least it's a building. Most of that place is nothing. They literally are planning for almost nothing to be there. So you know, some urban form is appreciated. The big flat plaza should go, though."

"I don't want to comment too much on it. That's the problem. Architects want to make art. They usually fail, but if you critique something, or even just react to it, you make it art. They love that. They want to rub that reaction in your face. See, I made art! You loser, you don't like this building I failed at designing! It sucks."

"Well, I'd hate to see what happens if you critique me," she laughed.

"Oh, you're art anyway. You know you're pretty. That's like, old news. It's not very interesting to say."

"Well, I like you too," she said, pointedly.

"And I think you're an alien from outer space," he replied. "Out of this world. And for some reason, I think it's boring to mention that. You know, my brain is weird like that."

She kissed him. "What were we talking about?" she asked.

"Buildings. Plazas."

"We're so boring," she laughed, rubbing her eyes. "You're gonna make me lose my edge. I'm supposed to be pretty out there. Now I'm all peaceful and shit. Just hanging out with you. It's a different vibe."

"Am I boring?"

"Not boring. You just don't worry about stuff." Connor wasn't sure if that was true. "I'm like, wired. I have to calm myself down sometimes. Things roll off of you. Maybe you're making me more like that."

"You kind of blew up at that lady."

"Yeah, I did. But usually I would go back to my place and be mad about it. I'd sit on the couch and just think and be anxious. Now I'm here with you, and I don't have that pain in my chest. It's confusing."

"You're a confusing woman," Connor said. "Ma'am."

"Very funny," she said, running her fingers through her hair. "When did I get old?"

"You didn't get old. Not yet."

"I'm twenty-eight."

"Are you serious?"

She looked at him with a funny expression. "I never told you how old I am?"

"I'm not supposed to ask."

"No, you're not."

"You've lived like, a hundred more lives than me," he said.

"Okay, slow down! I'm not that old."

"If that's what I meant, I probably would have said something like that. I don't know if I've ever met a girl who's twenty-eight. I wouldn't know where to find one."

"They don't just show up at your job?"

"I guess they do. Or at least, when I had a job, that's what started to happen. Would you know anything about that?"

"That seems weird," she said. "I don't know anything about that."

"But actually – what have you been up to? I just, I don't know. I didn't think you were twenty-eight. I'm sorry. What does someone do between twenty-three and twenty-eight?"

"You know, my mom said, it's okay to try different things. So I did that. I mean, I failed a lot. I was a mail carrier to start with, but it hurt my butt to drive the mail van. I tried reselling vintage clothes, but it turns out you have to go to Goodwill and elbow out other resellers and the working poor and teenagers for the good stuff every morning, and that was too hard for me. I don't like getting up early, or doing things that feel like stealing. Well, I did shoplift a bit as a teenager, but I wouldn't call that a career. I did study planning in school. I have my degree, somehow. That was something I liked. Especially urban planning, and all that stuff. I just didn't want to get a job right away. I told myself I had some time to figure it out, and I guess I do. I didn't realize that it's harder to get back into when you're a few years out of school. The last thing I tried was I started a fashion blog, where I would do affiliate marketing on the stuff I wore. It didn't make me any money, and I hated working on the website. I ended up taking it down."

"You, fashion?"

"Hey, shut up. I have some fashion sense. What would you know about it?"

"I know a few things."

"Name one thing you know about."

He paused for a moment. "I can't really think of anything, just right off the dome like that. Or, I guess, I know about how to repair bicycles. I can be handy like that."

She was giving him that funny look again.

"Do you know enough to stop talking?" she asked, and pulled him close.

12

Vincent Reznor walked out of the hospital. No, that was wrong. Vincent Reznor left the hospital in a wheelchair pushed by his girlfriend, Mack. Strangely, he didn't feel any loss in independence, or any shame in being temporarily wheelchair-bound. If anything, it was a lot like skating, and it was cool to skate. It was also cool to vape. He raised his right hand in the air, and Mack placed a brand new, clunky-looking vape in his hand. He'd volunteered for a clinical trial where pain medication was administered via vape. The nurses had originally complained that he vaped in their presence, a violation of the hospital rules. When the doctor found out, he realized he'd be the perfect candidate for the trial. The treatment was theoretically for patients who had trouble swallowing pills, but nobody could accuse Vincent Reznor of being bad at taking pills—he was just great at vaping.

An unmarked black van came screaming around the hospital's pickup loop. The back doors of the van opened and men in tactical khakis and bulletproof vests came rushing out. They began lowering what looked like a wheelchair lift. Before Mack could react, the men nabbed Vincent from her and started wheeling him towards the lift.

"Yo, get off him! This is crazy! You're kidnapping him!" she shouted, struggling against the man who had grabbed her as well. They started to drag her to the back of the van, though she didn't need much convincing to go where Vincent was going.

"Get your hands off me!" she shouted.

"Relax," the man said, his face stern. "We just want to talk with you. Nobody's in trouble. It won't be an hour."

"What's all this for?" she shouted, as she was loaded into the backseat of the van. There was a wire cage between her and the front of the vehicle.

The man took off his sunglasses and looked back at her through the cage. He looked like he could be someone's dad. "We..." he started, "don't really know any other way to bring someone in for questioning. They only train us on how to do it this way."

She could hear Vincent struggling in the back of the van, but the medication had had him pretty out of it.

"You know what he did," the man said. "Now you're gonna have to answer some questions, so we can decide if you're going to Guantanamo. Don't be stupid."

"I don't know what the hell you're talking about!" she said. She kicked the cage a few times.

The man pressed a button on the dashboard, and instantly an electric shock came through the back seat of the van. Mack screamed in pain, and almost flopped onto the floor. "Please chill out," the man said. "You're being extremely not-cool right now. I don't like to have to shock you. Every time I shock you, I have to fill out a form afterward. So don't make me do that."

"What kind of fucked-up police car is this?" she shouted. "I'm chill, dude, I'm chill. Clearly kicking the stupid grate doesn't work. Whatever. It's not like you expect to get shocked in a police car."

"Have you heard of the 100-mile zone?" he asked.

"The what?"

"You know what, never mind. That's enough for one day. Let's head to the office."

The front dashboard of the van had a large screen where the dashboard might have been on a regular car, bigger than most laptops. The cop (was he a cop?) hit a few buttons, pulling up a webform. "What's your name?" he asked.

"I'm not telling you."

"Okay," he said. He checked the box named 'John Doe', which was next to 'Jane Doe' and 'Sock Doe'. He kept one hand on the wheel, narrowly dodging pedestrians and cyclists as he went. The digital keyboard was sticky, not always picking up his input. He seemed to make a few typos as he filled in the reasons for him shocking her.

"Okay, let's send this one out," he said. A whoosh sound came from the dashboard. An animation played on the screen, and then a green checkmark showed. "Great news. A federal judge approved my use of force. Looks like we got away with this one, girl who has no name!"

For some reason that didn't make her feel better. The van bumped through the squares and streets of the town that was nowhere at all, that she called home. She wasn't sure why people called it nowhere. There were things to do, people to see. Music on the streets. Besides, Vincent was there. He was her hero and shit. After a half hour of driving, she was led out of the van to a nondescript building.

She was led through a cinderblock hallway and sat in a room with two office chairs, and a folding table between them. The officers quickly departed. She looked around. The room had two-foot square acoustical ceiling tiles at a standard 9-foot height. A four-foot by two-foot fluorescent light flickered above her head, casting an uninviting white glow on the room. A square plaque diffuser supplied one hundred cubic feet of air to the room with each minute that passed. The floor was polished concrete. She gripped the arms of her chair and spun around. She was pretty sure she hadn't done anything wrong. She broke the law occasionally, sure, but not in ways these guys would care about. These guys weren't the weed police.

The man who walked in had attractive gelled hair and a made-up sensibility about him. He wore a brown blazer over a gray t-shirt that said "IT'S ME" on the front, with a drawing of a bear. A round container of synthetic tobacco left a noticeable circle in his pants. He smiled at her and flipped the chair so it faced the opposite way, and sat in it, resting his arms on its back.

"Hey there," he said. "You can call me Yakub."

"No dress code at work?" Mack said.

"Well, they let me do what I want. Is it bad?"

"No, it's fashion."

"That's right. It's fashion." He snapped his fingers, and pointed at her. He removed his hat, slicked back his hair, and put it on backwards. "Listen," he said. "I just need to know what you and your friend did. That day."

"Boyfriend," she said.

"That's not what he said." Yakub smiled.

She shook her head. "I know him. He wouldn't say jack about dick to you. Especially not about me."

"You gotta tell me. Otherwise, it's gonna be a lot worse." Was that a neck tattoo that he had, poking out from under his t-shirt?

"Nothing happened. That's the whole story. I don't know what the hell you're bringing me in for. I'm a model citizen. I don't even hurt cats."

"You don't hurt cats?"

"No. Sir," she spat.

"Anything else you want to say to me?"

"Yeah, I want a lawyer. L - A - W - E - R. You hear that, you stupid asshole? That's right. Now get outta here."

"That's not a magic word, honey," he said. "We have twenty-four hours together, in this beautiful place. We actually got a psychiatric hold for you two. Not that we needed to, but the paperwork was shorter. You're not getting a lawyer, because... oh let me check." He pulled a sticky note from his pocket. "You were yelling incoherently in the hospital, threatening staff and patients... oh this one's good. You defecated through the sunroof of our van. The van doesn't even have a sunroof. Do you think the judge will catch that one? Anyway, I don't want to be mean. I want to leave you in one piece. So you can just tell me what happened, and you'll be on your way."

"You just made all that shit up.".

"Who's to say? That's my lived experience. Who are you to question it?" Damn, his lived experience. He may have gotten her on that one. The detective got up, and pushed his rolling chair into her table, bumping it lightly. He walked out the door, not saying anything further.

In the next room, Vincent Reznor was relaxing in his wheelchair. The detective walked in. Vincent noticed his fake Jordan sandals and his stupid wristwatch. "Nice J's, bro," Vincent said.

"Oh, thanks man," the detective replied, kicking the sandals against the wall to shake the dust off of them. "It's casual Friday. Name's Yakub, by the way."

"Is it even Friday? I don't know what day of the week it is anymore." Vincent stretched and tried to wiggle his toes. They moved but were still weak. He wanted to be up and moving soon, if only to make a daring escape.

Yakub checked his phone. "It's certainly a day of the week. We'll come around to Friday at some point. Anyways, I want to know what put you in that chair."

"Well, that part is easy," Vincent said. Yakub's ears perked up. "There was a big explosion, and there was some, uh, neurotoxin in the air, and it knocked me down pretty good."

"That's it?" Yakub asked, throwing his hands out in the air. "Let's take some responsibility here. You kids, you're all, well this just happened. Sorry, Dad, some tomato sauce got on my shirt. Sorry, Dad, some poop ended up in my underwear. Sorry Yakub, I'm leaving you for your cousin, he's the crueler, sexier version of you. Whatever. Let's hear it this way: I made the train derail. I thought it would be funny. I didn't think so many people would get hurt. And then we can even get into an apology if you like."

"What's the train got to do with me? I'm the victim here, man! I got the whole neurotoxicity thing going. Where the hell is my vape! I don't remember shit, man, I just woke up in the hospital one day, and now you took me to some stupid secondary location. I wasn't involved in any of it."

"Oh right," he said. "I almost forgot." Yakub wheeled a cart with a TV on it across from Vincent. He pushed a VHS tape into it and fiddled with the player until it turned on. "I can't believe they still make these," he said, banging the side of the TV twice. It flickered to life. The television played gray CCTV footage of an empty road, with the train tracks crossing the image. After thirty seconds of stillness, the gate arms began to lower.

"Did you see this happening?" Yakub asked. "The railroad crossing arms mean, don't go there, you'll get hit by a train. I think even children know that."

"I don't even know where this is," Vincent said.

The video continued. In just a few frames, Vincent flew into view on his boosted board. He was probably going thirty miles per hour. The wheel appeared to catch on the tracks, and he flew through the air before tumbling and rolling on the pavement. Damn, Vincent thought. That was quite a spill. It was hard to come back from a fall like that. That same moment, the train's locomotive, in the grainy black and white of the CCTV, slid elegantly off the tracks as it broke the skateboard, and continued down the road. It seemed businesslike in the way it continued down the road as if nothing were amiss. It plowed into a nearby building, obliterating it. The railcars followed one by one, bending and twisting as they were forced to come to a stop, jackknifing across the road and on top of each other. The footage started to stutter and skip, as smoke filled the screen. A few frames showed Vincent crawling away before the screen switched to pure static.

"That's trippy, man," Vincent said. He knew he should probably feel scared. He didn't. He was here right now, and didn't remember a bit of whatever was happening on the screen. He couldn't comprehend that the guy in the video and the guy sitting in that interrogation room were the same person. "This is like a movie," he said. "I did all that?"

"You did, Vincent," Yakub said. "The thing I just can't figure out is, why you did it."

"Shit, I mean it looks like an accident to me," Vincent said. "Those tracks will get you. You know, that's a freak occurrence though. I go home that way every day. Check the tapes. Usually, I just glide right over. Every day, I go that way across the tracks. It ain't a conspiracy." He was telling the truth. Mack was always telling him to be more careful on the board.

The detective leaned over the table and frowned. "This is serious stuff, kid. I can tell you're a good kid. Maybe you made a mistake, you thought it would be funny to throw something on the tracks, see what happens. You didn't think it would go so wrong. I mean, who could picture it? A whole neighborhood turned to ashes. Neurotoxins in the air. You know, my boss, he's a very difficult man. I know he's gonna watch the tape back later and slap me for that, but you know, it makes him good at his job. He's breathing down my neck, he says, this kid is probably some sort of terrorist. Maybe even a bio-terrorist, which is worse. Now, I am not an expert on all things terrorism, but to me, you know, me sitting across from you, talking like two guys should, I don't think Muhammad Bin Salmon is signing your paychecks. I don't think the FSB or Mossad is, either. I think that Jimmy's Unquestionable Seafood does, that little dive you work at. But I need you to meet me halfway here if we're ever gonna cut a deal. Do you understand me?"

"Salmon? Like the fish?" Vincent leaned back, stretching.

"That's what you took away from it? Asshole kid. I'm trying to cut you a deal!"

"Salman. Pronounce it right, man. I watched a documentary about that shit. Anyways—there's no deal that we are gonna cut, because I didn't do shit, and you know I didn't do shit." Vincent leaned against the table, his legs shaking with weakness, his voice firm. "Look at that stupid video you got on your stupid tape. Yeah, you caught me falling over like some Jerry. It blows that the train crashed. It hurts my heart, man. You think I didn't get knocked flat by that whole thing? I was right there! I'm in a chair dude! I was knocked out for days, man, an actual coma. With neurotoxins and other bullcrap in my brain. You're lucky I'm not a zombie at this point, I seriously think, you know, a bit more neurotoxin and I'd have just started biting people. Just gnawing on you, bro, making a meal out of you. I woke up with this girlfriend too, and I never even went steady with a girl like that before! You know, she is cool, but I never had to do something like that in my life, and now I got to. You think I wanted to do all that?" Vincent's vision started to go blurry, and he laid back in his chair. He took a few deep, gasping breaths. The pain was coming back. Where the hell was his vape?

"Dude, you're a mess," Yakub said, putting his head in his hands. "You've gone all pale. All that just to screw with me."

"I'm not screwing with you!" he shouted, but it provoked a coughing fit. He leaned on the armrest of his chair and shut his eyes, trying to recover. He wondered what he could have done to deserve all this. It wasn't like he was some bad guy. He had love for everyone, he thought. He didn't mean to cause any trouble. He barely paid attention as the detective left the room, slamming the door behind him. The room started to spin. Vincent Reznor laid back in his wheelchair and dreamed.

13

Stirbert, Nigel, and Pablo sat against a brick wall, staring at another brick wall across from them. Stirbert was bouncing a tennis ball off the far wall and watching it roll back to him. A rat that had been trying to get at a nearby dumpster was frightened by the sight of it and scurried away. The sun was out—it was usually out, lately, regardless of if things were good or bad. Sometimes Stirbert wished for a bit of rain. He also was pretty sure that it was bad that it rained less. He decided he should check later.

"So, you ever going to tell us what happened?" Pablo asked.

Stirbert reached up and felt the bandage across his nose. Touching it stung. He thought of the blow the angry man gave him, how it made him feel. "It wasn't anything," he said. "I think he called me a queer or something like that. It's not even that bad to be called that anymore. You know, I should let that go. But it got to me for some reason. So I swung at him."

Pablo cocked his head to one side, then the other. "Well, you were very brave to yell at him like that."

Stirbert thought of his father. Always with a comment, calling him stupid things that people didn't really even call each other anymore. Stuff that was not even offensive to most people because it was strange. His favorite was Pansy. You're such a Pansy, won't work at your father's business. You can't even pick up a can of paint, you're not strong enough to lift it. He liked queer as well. However, acting out just because your father was mean or said something you didn't like as a kid was stupid. It was too predictable. So Stirbert decided that he wouldn't say that—it would be too obvious a solution, and the guys might not believe him. "Yeah you know, it just felt good to yell at the guy." That much was true. "Guys like that have always pissed me off. I wanted to put him in his place a bit. I guess that makes me a bully."

"You're half his size," Nigel said. "It would be lousy to name you a bully."

"I should just be the bigger guy," Stirbert said. "Metaphorically speaking."

"But who is the bigger man? What does that mean, you know, under this, eh... capitalist realism?" Pablo said. He was going to get weepy again, Stirbert could tell. He actually liked the rants—they were funny, and he had something good to say at least some of the time. They'd been happening with increasing frequency ever since the disaster, though. "The man who allows the physically stronger man to step on him, what will he do when one of his fellow workers is under the boot of his boss? He might allow that too. Or maybe, worse, he would help the worker, but not himself, because he thinks he's not deserving of help. Well, this is worse. I would call this man sexually frustrated. Bigger or smaller, that doesn't even come into the equation." Pablo waved his hands and pounded the table once.

"Okay, Pablo," Nigel laughed. "That's enough."

"I mean, what is this?" Pablo continued. "Taking the high road. Whatever! I will be kind to people. Yes, it's my duty to be kind. It's what my mother would want anyway. I don't need more rules beyond that."

"Must be easy to be you," Stirbert said. "No rules."

"No, not easy at all. Because then you have to decide for yourself, Stirbert, my young friend," Pablo clapped him on the shoulder. "I have given you the gift of free will. I give you permission to name that man as naughty in your sight, and smite him. If you live by rules, then you just interpret the rules to decide how you should treat that man. In this case, maybe the rule says you should just take it and not fight back. I say, decide for yourself, but be kind when you can. Maybe you did the kind thing by calling him those names. It's not my business. Maybe he's had a change of heart because of you; I cannot say."

Stirbert wasn't sure if his philosophy was coherent, but he thanked him for giving him free will. He figured Pablo was right in his own way—he should be his own man. He should be generous with people, but also not let them insult him. Or, did you have to let them, as long as you could move past it?

"Why are we sitting in a brick alley? Bouncing a ball?" Nigel asked. "How did we get here? We should be having a pint. I'd settle for a hot dog even. Do we even have those anymore? Were they all lost in the fire?"

"Stirbert got sick last time we had a dog," Pablo said, "and he's too young to drink."

Stirbert turned red. "Not that young," he said. "I'm nearly there. Besides, who took the fun out of life for you two? Now you're my parents? We can't go get some beers from the gas station?"

Pablo's eyes widened. "Who is this guy?" he laughed. "The Stirbert I know probably died and has been replaced. Whoever you are, impostor, go back to your alien planet, and leave us alone! Beer! Can you believe it? The kid wants beer."

"Fuck off," Stirbert said. He wasn't sure what was making him more and more comfortable with speaking up. He reasoned that he might have had a head injury.

"Oh, don't be such a knob, Pablo," Nigel said. "I asked for a beer first, anyhow. My arse is getting wet from sitting in this stupid alley. What the hell were we thinking?"

"I honestly can't remember," Pablo said. "It sucks here. I mean, what's that puddle? It's black colored. What could possibly be in it?"

"It's trash juice," Stirbert said, starting to get up.

"An abomination. Our excesses, you know, all of the packages we order. It is all juice at the end of the day, when we throw it out. And we insult it by calling it juice. It is our tears."

"That's enough," Nigel said, also standing up. He helped Pablo to his feet.

Pablo clapped his hands. "Enough of old, sad Pablo. We are going to the bowling alley! And maybe we can get you a beer there. Yes, no introspection today." He put his arms around the shoulders of Nigel and Stirbert, on either side of him. "And the lovebirds, they aren't invited. Just us lonely people, wasting our wages."

A short time later, Stirbert sat on a stool at the bowling alley. The carpeting was the classic deep blue, with red and yellow music notes strewn throughout it. The ceiling was high, with wide-format ceiling tiles laid parallel to the lanes. This alley was known for the amount of advertisements it contained. The pinsetter machine's sweeping arm had ads for local law firms and construction companies. The balls were sponsored, many by individuals. Stirbert caught one that was sponsored by a Mayor Johnson who'd been out of office for about ten years—it was known as the 'dick ball' by locals, and it had a strange weight issue that made it prone to going in the gutter. It was common to take an unsuspecting friend to the bowling alley and let them get 'dick balled', watching their bowls go in the gutter over and over, thinking it was their fault. Stirbert had been dick balled himself by Pablo, shortly after they'd met.

Pablo walked over to the lane with three milkshakes. "Sorry, no beers," he said. "It's too early in the day for them to sell it. So milkshakes it is."

The three of them leaned down close to the milkshakes to get a closer look. "This one's a real creamer," Nigel said.

"Glass has good rippling," Stirbert said. He lifted the glass with one hand. "Weight is excellent. Wow, feel the weight on this one," he said, handing it to Nigel.

"Wow, that's a heavy milkshake," Nigel said. "Here, take it back. I have my own."

He took a sip of his drink. "This shake is just bonkers," he said, licking his lips. "It's knocked me flat!"

Stirbert smiled. The milkshake game had always been funny, but it was something Pablo and Nigel typically did with Connor. He wasn't usually able to participate, partially because he didn't know how serious it was. The game was easy—just observe the milkshake as it was, say something thoughtful and funny about it, and you won.

"The advertisement, though, it hurts my heart," Pablo said. He pulled the straw from the milkshake and held it in front of them. Tri-City Reptile Sales, it said. "I hesitate to take you two gentlemen here, if only for this insult. An ad on a straw. How am I even to read it? I must pull it out like this, maybe lick it off, to even show it to you properly. Tri-City, what does that mean? Which three cities? Nobody knows. The British do not have this problem. They have specific names for these things."

Stirbert ignored him, and turned to the bowling kiosk to key in his and his friends' names. He put his name down first and got ready to bowl. He fingered a bowling ball, a ten-pounder. His fingers just barely fit in the holes, so much so that they scarcely were able to slide when he bowled with one. He walked right up to the lane, ball in hand, and thrust it down the boards. It spun right, then left, hitting the center pin. On that pin was a logo for some streetwear company. The pins crashed against one another carelessly, and the ball flew out the back and into the maw of the pinsetter. He curled his fists. One pin was left, the right pin. A neon light came on, and the pinsetter delicately lifted it from the ground, sweeping away the pins below. The ad for some personal injury law firm on the sweeping arm mocked him. His failure mocked him.

Still, he had another chance. Someone told him once—in bowling and in life, you always have two balls. Nigel and Pablo were lost in conversation, not seeing his work. He decided to aim more to the right. A twelve-pounder would do this time. His fingers fit into the holes, and he worried they might slip out during the bowl. The ball swung behind him, and then before him, before it launched into the air. This would be a high one. A third of the way down the alley, it thudded into the oiled wood. It spun to the right, but it didn't stop – it continued into the gutter. Unbelievable, Stirbert thought. The bowl should have been perfect. It picked up some speed in the gutter, rattling to one side and the other. As it was about to fall into the back, it caught an edge, kicked up to the left, and knocked the last pin over. A spare, from the gutter!

Stirbert spun around on one foot and pumped his fist. A shiver went down his spine. He felt like he must be glowing. "You don't mess with me!" He pointed with both hands at Nigel and Pablo. "Let's kick some ass. I'm ready. Let's go start something. They can break my nose again if they want. Your turn, Pablo. If you're done with all that yapping, that is." He sat on the stool and sipped his milkshake. The brothers exchanged a knowing glance. Stirbert had figured something out—nobody knew just what, though.

14

Connor opened the door of the Stinky Rat with a kick and held it open. In walked Kara, Nigel, Pablo, and Stirbert. It had been a while since they'd all gotten together, much less been able to sit down in their favorite diner, but the group chat had agreed that it was time they'd sat down and discussed things. It was eight in the morning, and Pablo looked like he had to have been dragged out of bed. The birds were still chirping. Connor could see over the bar, past the waitress, and into the kitchen. A couple skinny stubbly line cooks were already slinging pancakes and hash, summoning clouds of steam, smoke, and grease that were captured by the kitchen hood and exhausted onto the old streets, warning the world that it was breakfast time. This was the kind of restaurant where you didn't bother being seated by a host—you just sat down, and hoped someone would see you. People were good at waiting tables in this town. It was something you knew you could make a living doing. There was no shame in making a living.

They slid onto the cushioned red seats of the booth. Kara sat beside him, her leg brushing against his. A moment of physical contact, a stray glance—those moments were something he craved. Sometimes the tension could be better than the real thing. The floor had been mopped that morning, and his sneakers squeaked uncomfortably on the floor. Connor pulled his backpack onto his lap and pulled out five pieces of paper, distributing them to the group. He'd photographed and printed copies of a flier he'd seen posted on a few different lamp posts around town. He held the original in his hand. Printed in full color, the title was crimson, and it read: Nothing: An Urban Park Dedicated to Those We Have Lost, and a smaller subtitle under it: Notice of Public Meeting: Draft Environmental Impact Statement. Taking up most of the page was a rendering of the project area. It was mostly bathed in green, the kind of green that could only be produced by a computer, showing fields with choice tree plantings, and walking paths between. In the corner was the familiar spaceship-esque building, though on this particular drawing, it was silhouetted in black, masking its form, with a white question mark in the center of it. A thought bubble pointed to it, with the text, "Make your voice heard!" it read. There was a list of amenities below, in black, underlined font, advertising acres of 'open space', as well as the benefits to parking, increased road capacity, and the planned memorial.

"It's like they bombed the place," Kara said. She traced her finger along the city at a bird's eye view. "Building, building, building... it goes on like that. And then there's nothing at all."

"They are really calling it 'nothing'?" Nigel said, rubbing his eyes. "Who would want to have nothing?"

Pablo flipped his page over. "I'm choosing not to interact with this foul media," he said. "I blame you, Connor, for bringing it into my field of view." Stirbert shrugged and flipped his own page over too.

"See, this is the problem," Connor said. "Right now we are being reactive. We have been reactive. We see this stuff go down, and we just try to process it. Okay, that's fine. But like, we need to do something. We need to take that next step. Let's figure out how to stop this."

Kara produced some pens from her pocket. He'd rehearsed it this far with her—it had been her idea to give a bit of a call to action, but they weren't sure what the action might be. "Let's all flip the page over," he continued. "You know, let's throw out some ideas. See what sticks. What made the west end of town special? Why should it be kept? We should try and make this argument to people. I mean, if we can get everyone on our side, there's no way they can do it, right? Once they see."

Stirbert stared at the blank page, and set his pen down. "I mean, it's the music right?" he asked, his eyes scanning the group. "Junk is what it's about. The noise, the culture, the basements. I mean, my dad hated the stuff, he never let me go to shows when I was a kid. But now, I try to go. It's part of why I'm still here. They want to kill Junk."

Pablo nodded. "Our friend is right," he said. "Noise, vagrancy, crowding. Those are all the things the councilor lady was railing against. People coming together. They want to take our soul away."

Was it just the music? As the table discussed, Connor thought back on his life growing up in a place that was kind of nowhere. The last time there'd been a show, the house it was in was falling down. He heard they ended up condemning the place just days later. There used to be music most any night of the week; if you wanted, you could spend all your evenings getting your ears blasted by sentimental indie rock. Now, the same social pages that boosted those performances posted pleas for assistance for musicians who lost their homes.

"We could do a fundraiser?" he asked.

"Everyone's doing a fundraiser," Kara replied. "This town has turned into one big fundraiser. Isn't there anything better we can do?"

"Maybe we could do a benefit concert," Stirbert said. "Get the bands together out in the field, do a whole day-long thing, ask for money. Tell everyone, this is the very last one, unless you guys help us stop this."

"It's not a horrible idea," Pablo said.

"I like that," Kara said. "I like it a lot. We can show them what they're missing. But we can't call it a benefit, we're not an old person charity. We're trying to change something, make something happen."

"How do you cause something to happen?" Stirbert asked. "That's a silly way to phrase it. How does anything happen? They just do."

"We'll have to find out," Kara said. "What bands do you guys know? We can write them all down, see who is still around, and start working the phones…"

It went on like that for a while. The more she pushed for the idea, the more the guys seemed to like it. Their most daring idea, at Pablo's insistence, was not to host the concert at a local park or at a regular music venue, but outdoors, in the cleared rubble of the neighborhood. He had used some embarrassing language to describe it, something about a phoenix rising from a basement, but the others agreed it could draw attention to the issue. The construction work was winding down in the area. It was starting to look less like piles of burnt buildings and more like a gravel moonscape. Nobody would care if they were out there. Connor just hoped that they could make someone care; it seemed as if nobody did.

15

"I think this could work," Kara said. She and Connor were walking to where one of Connor's friends was staying. He was a bassist for one of the bands they hoped to invite to the concert. The clouds ate the blue from the sky and the two lovers held each other's hand, a connection between their arms that went to their insides and ate at them there, too.

"Yeah, I know," Connor said. He kicked a rock.

"What's that supposed to mean?

"Sorry, I said the wrong thing. I mean, I hope it works. It's going to be hard."

"Yeah," she frowned. "But it's not like we're up to much else."

"No, we're not. It will be nice to get everyone together. You'll get to meet some of my friends."

"How long have I known you? A few weeks? You keep inventing new friends for me to meet," Kara said. "They keep spawning in."

Connor laughed. "You know, I just don't need to see someone a lot to feel close to them. Sometimes all you need is to maintain that connection. Someone has a positive memory of you, you reach out once a year, and when you need it you can get help from them, or maybe you can help them if they need something. It helps you keep a larger network."

"I can't decide if that's sweet or cynical," she replied.

"Who's to say I'm not doing the same thing to you?" Connor said, taking both her hands in his. "Making you part of my network?"

Kara let go of his hands and continued walking.

"Do you have any siblings?" Connor asked. He tried to thread his hand into hers again, and she accepted it willingly. "I don't think I ever asked."

"I have an older brother," Kara said. "He's a lot older than me."

"How's that work?"

"I don't know," she said. "We don't talk much. I don't even know what he does for work."

Connor thought she might ask about his siblings, but she didn't. She grabbed his arm with both of her hands as they crossed the road. The time he'd almost been run over had worried her, and now she made a point to guide him across the street like he was blind. It made him feel younger than he was, but he didn't mind. It was good to be looked after.

"Okay, here's the rundown," he said. If he were a detective he might have pulled out a notepad, but he wasn't. "This guy is Henry Slender. That's not his government name, I don't know what his real name is. He plays bass for the Nopes."

"The Nopes?"

"Yeah. They are a pretty cool band. They made the I Don't Want It EP and the I'm Not Doing That EP, those both are pretty transcendental stuff. They have been refusing to release anything since, but you can see them at shows. Anyway, this isn't his house, it's the house of his girlfriend, whose name is Maura. She is nicer than him, so we should probably try to convince her first. They're always together."

"Okay, and I'm going to do the talking?" Kara asked.

"Yeah, that would help. I mean, I'll introduce you guys."

The hotel rose four floors high, with a faux brick facade on the first floor and vinyl siding on the others. It had a stately flat roof and windows with small cornices. The dropoff loop in front of the building seemed so tight as to not permit any actual cars to pass through, more of a vestigial artifact of hotels needing to have such features, like the useless pelvis bones of a whale. Connor was pleased that the front doors were automatic, sliding open with the sound of rubber rubbing against glass.

The hotel room was on the first floor. There was no sign of life anywhere in the hotel; nobody was walking around, there was no noise coming from the rooms. There hadn't been a front desk person. Connor knocked on the door, and there was no response. He knocked a second time, and it flung open. The man that opened it had long, curly hair, and a round nose. He looked like he'd just woken up.

"Connor?" he said. "You couldn't text me?"

Connor looked down at the paper he was holding and back up. "This is kind of an in-person conversation," he said.

He shook his head. "What's going on?"

Kara reached out to shake his hand. "Hey, I'm Kara, it's nice to meet you," she said, smiling. He took her hand, looking skeptical. "I assume you are aware of the project going on in the west end? They are calling it Nothing?"

"Yeah, I heard of it." He crossed his arms.

"Well. We are, obviously, opposed to the project. We think that they should rebuild the neighborhood instead of destroying it. And we want to see what we can do to show public opposition to it, so we can put a stop to it. We also want to help displaced musicians such as yourself. So, this October, we want to hold a concert, with all the best Junk bands from the area. We are going to plan the whole thing; you guys just have to show up, with your instruments. We would really appreciate your support."

The man looked at her for a moment, not smiling. "No, I can't do that. I'm busy." He started to shut the door.

"Wait!" Kara said, surprised. "Why not?"

"No... I just can't," he said. He closed the door, leaving Connor and Kara alone in the blank hallway.

They walked down the hall, and Kara was miffed. "His room was filthy," she said.

"What, it's full of junk? Never met a Junk artist?" Connor laughed. "You're lucky I have no musical talent. My room would be worse."

"Oh I've dated a bassist before," Kara said. "Don't worry about that, I know. Doesn't make it better."

"A bassist?"

"Yeah. Once we went on a weekend trip to Manhattan together. We walked by the diner that they go to in Seinfeld, the one over on Columbia's campus. They never filmed in there, it was just used for exterior shots. You know the one. Anyway, he had his friend who was from the area hide in the bushes with a bass, and when we walked by, he handed him the bass, and he played the Seinfeld theme for me."

"That sounds awesome," Connor laughed. "Seems like a cool guy. I've never seen that show, though."

"It was not awesome," she laughed. "It was the worst day of my life!"

The next person Connor had on his list to talk to lived down the hall. This one, he hoped, didn't make a living by writing songs about saying 'no'. He pulled the list of rooms and names on his phone. "Okay, this one is Joey, last name unknown. Lead singer for The Savings Banks."

"That's a great band name," Kara said.

"Yeah, he's a good dude. We go way back. I think he'll totally go for it. Just roll with that same pitch as before."

Connor knocked on the door, and it was opened within seconds. "Connor!" the man said. He was wearing a patterned dress shirt and Adidas sweatpants. "What can I do you for? You couldn't have texted me?"

"Yeah, I think I may have, but didn't get a reply. Don't worry about it, it's cool," Connor said. He felt bad lying, but he also knew that Joey didn't save contact names in his phone.

"Oh man, I'm sorry. I must have missed it," Joey said, facepalming. Connor knew that the gesture was exaggerated for effect, something Joey had to do a lot when confronted with the fact that he had forgotten something. He peered over his shoulder into the hotel room, since Kara had mentioned it. It was definitely messy, with clothes in piles on the floor, but it wasn't filthy. There were no takeout containers or cups of goop left out.

Kara reached out to shake his hand, and he eagerly accepted. "Hey, I'm Kara, Connor's friend," she said. Connor wasn't sure if he should be mad that she didn't say 'girlfriend' or not. He figured she was just modern. "First of all, we're big fans of your band, the Savings Banks. You guys have some really out there stuff going on, it's very impressive. Anyway, there's a proposed project over in the west end of town. They're calling it Nothing. They want to basically replace the neighborhood with parkland and parking lots. Connor and I, and a lot of other people, believe that they should rebuild the neighborhood how it was, or at least pretty similar. And we want to show some public opposition to the project. We want to hold a concert, with bands like yours, the best Junk bands from around town, and the proceeds will also go to help people that lost their housing, like you. We are handling the planning; all we need is for you guys to show up, hopefully with your instruments. We would really appreciate your support."

Joey blinked a few times, face blank, as if trying to take in the paragraph she'd just spoken. "So it's like, a concert, and we'd get money for it?" He scratched his stubble.

Kara laughed. "Well, the money is incidental," she said. "We are taking donations. And the money will go to the bands. But it's not really about the money, it's about the cause."

Joey frowned. "You know, I'd really love to do it," he said. "But I can't. I just don't think I could get the guys to agree to it. Yeah, it's gonna have to be a no. Sorry."

"Do you mind saying why?" Kara said. "I mean, you guys play shows all the time, or at least you did. This one is for a great cause. We'll need your help if we want to save the neighborhood."

"It's complicated," he said. "I shouldn't really say. If I was going to say something, I'd say that you guys might get better luck trying to put a show together if you talked to Green Gary. But I've already said too much—anyways, I have to feed my girlfriend's cat, and before I do that, I need to return some videotapes, if you know what I mean. Just kidding. Alright, bye guys." He shut the door.

"Green Gary? Who the hell is that?" Kara asked. " What a weird dude, and a messy room too."

Connor happened to know who Green Gary was, and why they had to talk to him. He wasn't sure if they were ready.

16

Pablo held the heavy bucket of wheatpaste for Nigel, who dipped a freshly printed poster into it. He pressed the paper against the telephone pole and flattened it with his hand to make it adhere. He unclipped a paint roller from his belt, flattening it the rest of the way, the excess paste squirting onto the ground. Pablo scraped the drippings into the gutter with his boot.

"Do you think it will work?" Pablo asked as he started down the street.

"I'm not sure," Nigel replied. "But the girl is right. We have to try something. It's not like we're that busy."

"I think the painting business might start up again," Pablo said. "Stirbert's father, probably he's angling for a contract to paint that new park. There will be some walls, some fences, it's all easy work. But of course, it is at the cost of your soul."

"I would probably go paint somewhere else if I had to do that."

"We'll be okay. We will have to leave this place. Maybe I'm too old for music. I should be shopping at upscale grocery stores and going to breweries, not watching college students play guitar. At least, this is society's plan for me."

"I don't much want to move. It's not so bad here. At least it wasn't. Moving across the ocean is bad enough."

"You could go back to England."

"I'm not going to rotten old England."

"No, you're not."

And so they walked down the street, in the town that was in nowhere particular, within the free country that they had no place in. A single-floor industrial building on that street was a frequent target of graffiti, and the content of the wall changed frequently. This time, there was writing in favor of the current war. Pablo didn't care as much about the war as some of his friends, but he knew that this particular graffiti had no place on this wall. One should vandalize because the thing they wanted to say was implicitly against the status quo. If a potential vandal had the government's backing, they should probably just run ads on TV. He suppressed the urge to rant about this to Nigel; instead, he just indicated silently that he should put a poster up over it. After Nigel put up one, he waited with the bucket instead of moving. Nigel grinned and pasted four more on the wall.

They found this more fun than just targeting noticeboards and street lights. Graffiti artists went over one another all the time, that was part of the gig, and nobody could or would get mad about it. So they'd find an inscription they found annoying, pithy, or offensive, and throw one of their own posters over it, which turned out to be amusing. Sometimes they'd be able to edit letters out of words to say something silly, and this was the greatest pleasure of all. Stirbert had the idea to make an email address specifically for the concert to collect inquiries. He'd also offered to set up a website, which he was working on from his apartment. Pablo had agreed, as long as the website would have a blog; he'd always wanted to have a blog, somewhere to put all his long thoughts into. His thoughts were growing longer than ever, now that he had a highly salient cause to write about.

"And you wouldn't go back to Ecuador?" Nigel asked.

"Hey, I'm not some immigrant, like you!" Pablo laughed. "I'm a real boy. Gosh, I don't know. I miss my parents and my grandparents. I don't know why they moved back, I wouldn't have done that for any reason. I want to get some money together to visit them, but I'll never be able to do that just painting. And I've accepted that. Society has a way of making you into part of its machine, and that's fine, that's something I am used to accepting. Now things seem even further away."

Nigel began pasting another poster on a wall. He tried eating some of the wheatpaste off his finger, but spat it out, finding it gross. "You got us," he said. "You definitely have us."

"I know, my friend," Pablo said, and for once, had nothing more to say.

"I've thought about England a lot since the explosion," Nigel continued. "I don't think they have stuff like that over there. I know that sounds weird. Yeah, sometimes something burns down. But they don't have these Chernobyl-style disasters there, things are too buttoned up. Here, the disaster is over in a day, and loads of people get hurt. In England, it's like it's embarrassing to have American-style disasters, so they won't, but then they'll try to starve as many orphans as possible to fix the GDP, and that's considered sensible. God save that old man in his palace."

"Now look who's long-winded," Pablo said. He placed the bucket at his feet and pointed. "Would you look at this?"

They'd reached the end of the preserved portion of town and the edge of where the fire had reached. A dozen people were standing in a semicircle staring at the wall. Several were taking pictures with their phone, and some had large photographer-style cameras. Over his shoulder, Pablo could hear honking and saw that it was a news van trying to make its way to the scene. He and Nigel inched closer to the source of interest, the dirty white-colored wall.

Finally, he got the picture of what was there. "Seems another artist has been by," Nigel remarked. Stenciled in black paint, with crisp edges against the white surface probably touched up by a black marker, was what looked like a railcar in the process of falling onto its side. Several bright red heart-shaped balloons were shown spilling out of the side of the railcar. Strangest of all was what was below the balloons. Towards the ground, at the dirtiest part of the wall, there was a man, drawn strangely small, the size of one of the balloons. He was on his back, propped up by his elbow, looking up at the railcar and the balloons. The paint had been applied liberally and allowed to drip, giving the impression that he was beginning to melt.

"It's a tad on the nose, don't you think?" Nigel said. "The art isn't bad, though."

"Why is there love coming out of the train?" Pablo said. He frowned. "It was neurotoxin. Was that intentional?"

The crowd was beginning to grow around the wall. One police officer was backing people away who were getting too close, and another was rolling out caution tape to make a boundary. The news van had already birthed a reporter with a cameraman in tow, who was interviewing a smiling plump landlord. "Genuine art, in my own little logistics space!" he said. "Can you believe it? I've always been a fan of Stampy, and this just goes to show you that he goes where he's needed the most."

The smiling brunette reporter was standing on a milk crate to be on his level. The landlord was not dressed for TV; his white shirt had a few oil stains, and his jeans were not much better. "Do you have any plans for what to do with the art?" she asked.

"Well, I wouldn't want it to get destroyed!" he said, shrugging. "A genuine Stampy doesn't come around every day. Everyone should be able to enjoy this art. With the rain, the chemicals, well, we don't know how long this will last out here. So we will have to cut it out of the wall and have it sent to whatever museum will pay me a fair price for it. It's only fair. My property manager has already been sent to look for a saw that can cut concrete."

The reporter turned to the camera. "Well, there you have it, folks!" she added.

Nigel was in the process of looking up who Stampy was on his phone. "He's a Brit!" he muttered. "I had no idea about this guy. Is he popular with the kids?"

"Never heard of him," Pablo said.

"He does this all the time," Nigel said, showing Pablo some photos as he swiped through them. "He was at that fire in London, several of the wars that happened recently. He was even over at the Supreme Court when they were being disagreeable."

"And now here," Pablo said. "A disaster tourist?"

"People like the art," Nigel said. "Who am I to criticize? You'd just say if I criticize him, I'm making it more 'art' than it already is."

"He might call it raising awareness. But I'm not sure you could get any more aware of this than we already are. More helicopters is just what we needed right now." Pablo elbowed his way through the small crowd and snapped a photo of the art. He hadn't formed an opinion on the art but wondered if he could make posters with it to advertise the concert further. As Nigel and him walked away from the scene, he saw the next building. It was a three-floor brick building with a salon on the first floor, and apartments above, but that wasn't what Pablo noticed – the side of the building had a concrete wall where another building once stood. There were no windows, cornices, or other features cut into the wall, since it was intended to be shared with another building. It was completely blank. It was on the edge of the demolition area; it was likely that the building's sister was just demolished.

Pablo started to rock the bucket of wheatpaste up and down in his hands. He tapped it with his fingers, and tapped his foot as well. Nigel was looking up at the blank wall. His right hand curled as if he were already holding a paintbrush. Pablo broke from his stupor and started towards the direction they came from. He walked fast enough that the crowd broke to let him through, and Nigel followed, surprised at Pablo's speed. "We've got work to do, my friend," he said, a skip in his step. "What is it they say? A million things are happening, Nigel, that are so small, yet beautiful."

17

"I washed your shirt this morning," Connor said. He watched for her reaction, watching the hair fall in and out of her face. "I didn't mean to. It got mixed in with mine."

She grinned at him. "Thanks!" she said. She had a way of flipping her head one way and another. Looking here and then there, a reply given and withdrawn quickly. The chance acknowledgment of a moment.

She reached for the door, finding it already cracked, and swung it open. Green Gary sat on the middle level of a three-tiered cat tree, his legs crossed. An orange cat pawed at his lime-green sweatpants. Another cat was climbing onto his shoulders, which wore a sharp green blazer with feminine shoulder pads. He hit a button on the side of his bifocal glasses, causing the tint to vanish in an instant. Connor had no idea that was something bifocals could even do. Green Gary was like nobody else in town, and Green Gary knew people. So there they were, at his strange mercy.

"Please, have a seat," he said, his voice too high-pitched for his large stature. "Just not up here!" He laughed, but the sound he made sounded more like him breathing in air sharply a few times.

Connor stepped forward. "We were hoping to speak to you about–"

Green Gary raised his hand, indicating he shouldn't speak. He removed a pair of earbuds from his ears and clipped them into a small case. "Apologies," he said.

"I was listening to some sentimental indie rock. I'm sure you can relate. And yes, I know what you're here about. Nothing happens in this town without Green Gary knowing. When something happens that I don't necessarily like or enjoy, then I find out even faster. Make sense, or not make sense?"

Connor hadn't heard this speech in person before, but he was familiar with its content. Green Gary was a self-styled promoter for basement shows. He knew all the good places to play, the ones that were the most underground, the best places to go unnoticed, or be noticed, the dirtiest venues, and the cleanest too, if that's what your band preferred. Was a landlord trying to shut down your budding venue with accusations of noise, Green Gary probably knew the property manager and could get it straightened out. Some begrudgingly tolerated his presence, which involved a thirty percent take of revenue, a fascination with gadgets, and a difficult personality (to be diplomatic), but the truth was that anyone who wanted to make noise of any kind had to deal with him. He claimed an exclusive privilege over booking bands that he managed, and Connor knew that going around him would involve stepping on his toes. He'd tried his best, partly to impress Kara, he figured, and partly to see how serious the whole Green Gary thing was—and now he'd washed up on the man's doorstep, watching him pet his weird cats.

Gary stared at him, waiting for a response, then spoke anyway. "People say, oh, Green Gary is so mean! Green Gary won't let me knock on the bedroom doors of his musicians, he won't let me punch him in the gut, he won't let me step all over him, and use him as a toilet! He won't do it!" He started coughing, and raised his hand again, as an apology. He cleared his throat and started again. "But tell me your idea, in your own words, and I'll hear you out. Maybe this whole business has softened my heart so much that it grew three sizes."

Kara stepped forward. She was grasping one of her hands in the other. It looked as if her right hand was trying to stop her left from twitching. "What we want is to put on a charity concert," she said. Gary, saying nothing, switched his bifocals to sunglasses mode. She hesitated, and then continued. "To benefit musicians that have lost their homes. And we'd like to raise some awareness about the Build

Nothing project. We disagree with it; we think it's no good, obviously, and, I think you'd agree too, as someone who is, uh, so familiar with all the shows that went on there. I'm sorry if we upset you by talking to those bands. We didn't mean anything by it."

Gary looked at Connor and smiled knowingly. He knew who Connor was, at least enough to know that Connor should have known better. Connor smiled back and shrugged. Gary's smile slowly turned into a frown. "The destruction has been tremendous, there's no doubt about that," he said. "I look out my window, I press my ear to the glass—you know, my cats think I'm crazy when I do this—and I listen for the music. My music, that I have so delicately gardened and nurtured with my own milk of life. And I don't hear much music at all. I won't lie and say that my bottom line isn't hurting either. Gosh, it's like the old days again. When I came to this town, there wasn't any music, no, there wasn't. I need new basements, new bands. It's great that you want to put on a concert—I'm not sure what a concert does, practically speaking. It doesn't put anything back together."

Kara gulped. "Well, we'd like them to put the neighborhood back together. The way it was."

"It won't be the way it was," he said. "Those buildings were pre-war. Do you know what that means? Rats, roaches. Peculiar fire escape configurations. Ancient basements. And worst of all—the rent is cheap. What's in a new building? Sprinkler systems, double-loaded corridors, finished basements, containerized trash. Apartments that look like hotel rooms. I can't put on shows there, they'll call the cops. None of us will be able to afford to live there. I'm not even saying that that will be on purpose—new buildings cost money. I don't make very much money, contrary to what my detractors claim. Where's the place for me? I'll have to rent someplace and make it a venue. God, I'll have to make it a coffee shop during the day too, to pay the rent, probably. I fucking hate coffee!" He started coughing again and then wiped his nose on the sleeve of his blazer.

Connor was dejected. He knew the plan was an outside shot, but he hadn't thought much about what success would look like. Could they really put things back to the way they were? "But, the federal funds," he said. "The government is pouring millions into this project. I mean, why are none of us getting a piece of the pie? They could, you know, put some of us up more permanently, if there was money to go around. We've earned it. Plus, isn't this Nothing thing bad in itself? Shouldn't there be a kind of urban fabric going on? Cities have buildings."

"Buildings, no buildings. It's not my business," he said. "I'm no developer. I don't own a house. Gary's not getting any greener from any of those things, and that's fine by him. But you might be right about one thing," he said, scratching his thin beard. "Why are they cutting me out? Gosh, I mean, this art that has been destroyed, where's the memorials? The funding for artists? Don't they want to preserve and protect the legacy of the place that once was?" He hopped down from the cat tree and grabbed a notepad from his desk, and began writing. "We shouldn't be cut out of this deal. I should have—we should have—been consulted!"

He started to get excited. "Millions of dollars, you said? To build this waste of space urban park, maybe some parking lots for some nurses? I never met a nurse I liked, hate to say it. I was a medically expensive kid. Anyways..." he stopped and clenched his fist, considering it for a moment. He unclenched his fist, and looked up. "I'm in. And I want my thirty percent."

18

Vincent Reznor was back in a hospital bed, and all things considered, he didn't feel that bad. He didn't feel like he wanted to run away, stay put, or do much of anything. He felt like he was floating. It was nothing like vaping.

"He's waking up now?" someone said.

"Yes," the doctor replied, looking down at his clipboard. "I'll leave you two alone."

Vincent had a dozen things he probably could be asking, but he had learned by now that things were going sideways every day, and he shouldn't expect much of an explanation. That was a weird feeling, too. He was used to some control.

The man was wearing a light brown trench coat, with a white shirt and a black tie. His dark hair was gently gelled. He seemed oddly familiar. The gears turned in his head. At last, the realization came. Vincent coughed when he tried to speak, but finally managed to get a single word out. "Yakub..."

"I'm afraid so."

"Fuck you, Yakub! Curse you, asshole!" Vincent strained to get up, to give the guy a real piece of his mind, turn him into a Yakubian pancake, perhaps, but could not find the strength.

"Look, I'm sorry, man. Things got out of hand."

Vincent said nothing.

"Look, over at CBP, they're cowboys," he said. "They can't do the white glove treatment. It's only kidnapping. You're lucky that we had an accessible kidnap van available that day. Look, I can help you. I'm not those guys. I have my own thing going on. I have a lot of powerful ears that listen to my voice, 'cause they know I can find out the truth. You gotta help me tell them the right story."

"What the hell are you, then?" Vincent was not amused.

"I'm a detective," he said, clicking his tongue once. "We'll leave it there. Anyway, I was looking at you, you know, just waiting here for you to wake up, and I had a realization: You're not my guy. You're just too pathetic. I mean, look at yourself."

"Hey, man," Vincent replied. "It's not my fault."

"Not saying it is! No, not at all. But there's a problem with you not being the guy: Someone has to be the guy."

"There's no guy. There's no fucking guy. You saw the video. It's an accident."

"And yet we need one. Can you see my problem?"

"I don't see how it's my fucking problem."

"You seem stressed," Yakub said. "How about some refreshment?"

Yakub motioned to his bedside table. There, Vincent's vape lay in a plastic evidence bag. How could they have found it, after all this time? Vincent lunged for it and devoured it hungrily. Instantly, the fog cleared from his mind. He felt the blood return to his legs, his arms, his brain. His focus sharpened on the man. "Nah," he said. "I'm in the hospital, then I'm in the black site with some asshole, and now I'm back here in the hospital! I'm getting jerked around here. You got a little outfit on like it's fucking fashion week. Nah, I don't believe you, you comedian-looking creep. What do you want from me? Probably you're gonna ask to see my butthole or something!"

Yakub laughed, slicked back his hair, and scratched his nose. "You're a smart kid," he said. "We all want something. You know, I want to get married, settle down. Find a nice girl who I can treat right. But it hasn't happened for me—it's just so hard out there for guys like me. Like us?" he gave Vincent a quick look, and then shook his head, discarding the thought. "Anyways, we, you know—"

He waved his hands wildly. "—the government, we want something from you. But I think, you know, this could be pretty amenable for you. You're kind of in the, 'things happen to you' stage of your journey. We want to move you into the stage of accomplishing something, having some agency. Some type of deal that has mutual benefits for either of us. I don't think that's so bad."

Vincent was not sure what he was asking of him. "I'm no snitch," he said.

Yakub laughed again and slapped his knee heartily. "My dear Vincent, my bouncing, lovely boy. You don't have to snitch on anyone. I don't care who smokes grass. You don't need to pee in a cup. First, I need you to get better. We need you standing up and walking around. Yes, that much is in order, before you can think of the little favor you're going to do me. But first, I need to tell you a story. Can I do that?"

"You seem like a total asshole," Vincent said, lying back in the hospital bed. "But maybe if it makes you go away faster, I'll let you talk."

The man straightened his tie and stood. He looked out the window, and Vincent realized he had no idea what was out there. This place had all the characteristics of Mount Auburn Hospital, the local place to be, and the room he was in looked lived-in enough. He'd not stood on his own two legs for who knows how long, and he'd been in and out of consciousness, his once-strong body yanked from reality to unreality with as little thought as he gave to the vape hits he took regularly. He thought more about the window. The pale light showed itself on the faceless man. Was there a parking lot, with fractured pavement and mint toothpaste-green crabgrass bursting from it, a dozen SUVs vying for space, maybe some teenagers sitting on the curb, watching the day go by, the way he used to watch his life go by. The man didn't have to wonder about any of those things, Vincent thought. He wasn't sentimental at all. Vincent wasn't normally sentimental, either.

"Let's say there was a kid who tripped and fell. It happens all the time. This kid happened to be playing on his skateboard, and that skateboard fell on the train tracks. I don't think that's something that's entirely out of the question. You could imagine such a thing very easily. Anyways, the train comes rolling in:

Choo choo! The skateboard hits the wheel in just the right spot, and it goes off the tracks. The train goes up in a puff of smoke. Well, that's no good—someone has to pay for the train, someone has to pay for the house that the train ran into, and, oh dear, someone has to pay that kid's hospital bills. I feel bad for the kid, but I'm not paying it for him. You wouldn't want to pay either. Well, I could go on like this for a while. Does that make any sense?"

Vincent tensed. "I'm a grown man," he said.

The man snapped his fingers, turned, and pointed at Vincent. It could have knocked Vincent flat, were he not laid up in bed. "You are. Now you're getting me. Now let's say, a grown man is out there, on that unseasonably warm fall day. And he's playing with a children's toy—was that a skateboard, or was it an illegal variant of an e-scooter, unsuitable for a public way, much less a grade crossing? And now—millions, hundreds of millions in damage. People will want heads to roll. Just one head, they say! Someone to blame! Why not start with the 'grown man' at the center of it all?"

"You have been telling me I'm fucked all week," Vincent said. "Maybe I'm fucked—I probably am. That doesn't seem to move the dial very much."

He cracked his knuckles. "My point is, one way or another, people are going to figure it out soon. The convenience store owner—nice little man that he is—is getting some big offers for that footage. Every news station in the country will be happy to roll that footage on the eight o'clock news for a few nights. Your name will slip out—I think you're pretty well known for your little act with the skateboard, flying around town like that. You'll be recognized, no doubt. We have the resources to help you head this off, even protect you from liability—but you need to help us out."

"So what do I need to do? You've been ranting for like, five minutes now. Just spit it out already, or go find some other asshole to bother."

"It's not that much at all—we'd like you to make a few appearances, shake some hands, take a couple interviews. In support of the federal relief programs in the area."

"What? Relief programs?" Vincent said. "What's it got to do with me?"

"Well, we're trying to smooth things over," he replied. "There has been some grumblings, you know—some kind of out there stuff, mind you—that the spill was caused by the government in some way, and also some grumblings that what is going to be built on the cleanup site is inappropriate. It's stupid stuff, I know, if I seem vague it's because I don't want to bore you with it. My boss is convinced we need some sort of local kid to show that this is what the community needs and wants, a friendly face on the TV shaking the governor's hand. We want to get this wrapped up and done as soon as possible—people moving on. And who better to do it, than the guy who started it all?"

"Shoot, I mean, I always want to help the community out, I'm a big local guy," Vincent reasoned. "Still though, this all makes no sense to me. Why is there, like, opposition to that sort of thing?"

Yakub clapped his hand against the foot of Vincent's hospital bed. "That's my boy," he said, smiling. He laughed as he started to walk out of the room. "And for your question? I wish I knew. I guess some people just hate progress."

19

S tirbert stood watch over the night in the city. The street lights on this road had shorted out when the ward burned, so the dark was only broken by patches of light from the windows of a 24-hour laundromat and a McDonald's. The McDonald's flag flew at half mast, and it beat against its pole in agony. The crowd that Pablo and Nigel had talked about had disappeared, and it was only the friends and the mice and the rats of the city that were out this late, in this place. Rock dust lightly covered the ground. The wall where Stampy had made his statement had been sawed to pieces to remove the art, and the hole covered with a tarp. That part made him smile—what other painter could make someone cut open their own wall, just to preserve the art? The best any of them could hope for is that whatever they made wouldn't be painted over.

The debate had started in the late afternoon, and raged into the evening, almost to the time that it came to take their buckets out to the old building. What to paint? It should be bigger, better, art, yes, Nigel and Pablo had agreed. Pablo wanted to grace the wall with something more abstract, something with no figures or words at all, just form, a form that evoked some stronger ennui than Stampy could. Stampy's work was designed for the layman, he insisted, and by making something more 'fine art'-based he could do better. Nigel disagreed—if they were to upstage him, they should show that they could do his shtick better than he could. Some out-of-towner couldn't understand their struggles like they did. There should be a train again, but full of money, perhaps, to highlight that aspect of the issue—an idea Pablo found abhorrent.

There were no police around, and hardly any neighbors—the neighbors had had their homes burned down, and the police, well, there was hardly anything to police. That's all to say that Stirbert didn't think they were likely to be disturbed. He flicked on the floodlight, illuminating the brick facade in the night. The light spilled off the building and into the firmament, blotting out stars. Sorry everyone, no constellations tonight, he thought. Nigel and Pablo stood their own ladders against either side of the wall. They had done plenty of painting in their lives: bridges, walls, (plenty of walls), fence posts, gates, houses, roads, sidewalks, cars, little bits of art in their school notebooks as children—but never a mural. Pablo had remarked that despite his tendency to art criticism, he had forgotten to make much art in recent years. He'd studied the technique his whole life, just never had a reason to put it into practice.

The first step was to cover the wall with primer. This part was easy for them; it just involved coating the entire surface in the stuff. That part was just like old times. Stirbert remained on the ground level, painting anything he could reach without the use of a ladder. Conversation came easily, as it did on the jobs they were so familiar with.

"When someone's hunting in the woods, how do they avoid shooting other hunters?" Nigel asked. "Because if you think about it, you might mistake the hunter for an animal. A good hunter will disguise himself too, maybe wear camouflage. He or she might not look much like a person when they are in such a state. They might look like a deer."

"You don't know what a deer looks like?" Pablo laughed. "I think if I was going to shoot a deer, I'd make sure it was a deer."

"Well, shouldn't you keep your options open?" Nigel replied. "Maybe you find a deer, maybe a turkey, lion, ocelot—"

"Ocelot, brother? Where are you hunting, Africa?"

"Anyway, a hunter should have an open mind about what he's going to shoot. There could be surprises on the way. If you went out looking for a deer and there were no deer, that's a tough day. Anyway, it seems hard to do that and avoid shooting a person by accident. The British Museum has—"

Stirbert laughed. "Shut up, man."

"Yes, the open-minded hunter!" Pablo laughed. "My uncle would love to set you straight on that subject."

When the primer was applied, they stopped to let it dry, and Stirbert switched off the light. As their eyes adjusted, a few stars returned to the sky. The last few stars you could see, Stirbert thought. He used to go to his aunt's farm out in Pennsylvania, where the stargazing was better. He wondered if looking out at the stars made you smarter. It used to be that everyone could see every star, up until about two hundred years ago. Maybe it gave people more perspective on their place in the universe, and they'd act out less often. He favored the idea that someone could get used to anything if they were around it for long enough. The sky was what it was, and it followed you every night, and most of the time people did not look at it or acknowledge it, because they had other things you wanted to do. He'd read once that people who move to sunny places aren't much happier than people who live in cold ones—it's the change in temperature from cold and drafty to sunny and warm that makes people happy, not the climate itself. There is no supply of happiness stored in sunlight. But then again, sometimes he wondered if there was. He set an alarm for three hours from then, and lay with his back on the sidewalk, his backpack under his head. It was a great temperature to be outside, warm but with a cool breeze, and he felt snug with his fall jacket on. He tried to find the Big Dipper but had no success. Was it the wrong time of year? He knew so little about the stars. Soon, he was asleep.

Pablo had clearly not slept much when Stirbert awoke. He immediately brightened up when the alarm went off, encouraging Nigel and Stirbert to get up and work. They assented, but Stirbert had trouble stirring himself, foggy from sleep. His body had been ready to sleep the whole night away, not wanting to be woken up after just two REM cycles. He gathered his brushes and turned the flashlight back on. Realizing a mural was something beyond their experience but within their skillset, they'd googled around and saw the idea to put the form of the painting up in chalk before putting any paint up. Pablo's had started already, but his strokes did not resemble anything familiar, deciding to make his half of the wall an abstract piece of art—he preferred to turn the chalk on its side, for a wide, choppy stroke across the brick, shading in the areas he wanted painted in different colors with different markings. He worked silently this time, not telling jokes, or making fun of Stirbert or Nigel. He bit his bottom lip periodically. Nigel was up and down the ladder somewhat often, getting off of it to move it a foot left or right, so he could sketch out the entire outline of the shapes he wanted. He had put on his headphones, something he almost never did while he was painting regular exteriors. Stirbert had only seen Nigel wearing them in his private moments when he walked alone to work, or when he ran into him on lazy weekend mornings, reading a book outside his favorite coffee shop.

After a good long time, the sketch was complete on the wall, but Stirbert had trouble making out exactly what it was they were going for. Nigel had constructed several rectangles at various perspectives, two stick figures, but nothing resembling a coherent scene, at least to his eye. Pablo's side already seemed like art in itself, but whether it was good art or not was hard to say. He reminded himself not to pass judgment on it yet. He felt happy to not have to participate in the art-making—he could indulge in the success of it, but not have to make difficult decisions about it. He checked the buckets, the paint, and the ladders. Nobody had been by while he was asleep.

It was so late that it was in truth the early morning. With the floodlight taking his night vision away from him, Stirbert looked out at the tundra of the ruined neighborhood and saw nothing. It was like showering with the lights off—if he were to wave his hand in front of his face, he thought he might not see it. When you look at nothing, a visual static that can take its place. Shapeless shapes weave through the static and catch the attention of your subconscious, and your mind searches for them.

He imagined he was standing before the place where a multistory building once stood. Someone probably lived their life in that house, maybe up on the third floor. He saw a woman illuminated in the calm yellow light of a lamp making coffee in her kitchen, reading a book on the porch, arguing on the phone, hosting a dinner party. Having a complete experience. Then he imagined the house falling away, piece by piece, leaving her behind. She was floating in the air, sipping her coffee, reading her book, but with nothing around her. Then, she faded too. He could walk forward and walk under the place where the woman had been, but there would just be empty sky—she'd lived a life, twenty feet in the air above him, and now there was only air in that place. How could you keep a record of something like that, preserve it? Should he have a plaque installed in the ground? Nobody would care about such a plaque, maybe besides him. The woman might not think about her old place much either. She could be onto bigger and better things, or she could be buried somewhere in the endless gravel, ready to sprout flowers from her eyes and her hair that reach for the sky in the way she used to.

The color gold filled his sight. The sun peeked over the horizon, sending a beam of light against his eyes. He woke up right away, and his back hurt—when had he gone back to sleep? He dusted the dirt off of his jacket, his butt, and his shoes.

"Do you think babies understand what a sunrise is?" Pablo said. He sat to Stirbert's right, speaking softly, watching the sun rise. He had a paintbrush in his hand, and the paint had dried on the brush. "There must be an age where a baby can find it beautiful to see these colors. Maybe at the same age you realize how gray shit is."

Stirbert yawned. He was still trying to get his bearings back, but was thankful that they'd let him sleep. "A bear will look at the sunset," Nigel said, "if it is driven to it. They can sit like us humans do, butts on the ground, and watch it."

"What use is a sunset to a bear? It doesn't help it catch fish, or mate with other bears," Pablo said. "That much is nonsense to me. Though I can accept if I'm wrong and I've underestimated the bear."

Stirbert stood to his feet and stretched, turning around to face the wall. "Wow," he said. "This is huge!" It was huge. They'd managed to paint a mural across the full three stories of the building. It was primarily white and black, with red accents, a technique they'd cribbed from the stencil they'd found earlier. The morning sun spilled gold against the white bricks and paled the black bricks, whose texture cut through the painting and gave it bones and structure, catching shadows in their mortar and their cracks. The painting itself, Stirbert decided, was still on the nose. On Nigel's half, the diesel locomotive had been reimagined as a steam engine, puffing red bubbles of steam into the sky. As it moved to the right of the mural, it fractured into broken pieces of glass. Pablo's half of the painting was geometric, hexagons and octagons flying away from each other in different shades of black and white, the red accent this time being used to show where the shapes broke apart from one another as if quadrilaterals could have blood and bleed, too. It was extremely ambitious, but they seemed to have pulled it off.

"Well, what do you think?" Pablo said, clapping him on the back.

"It'll do," Stirbert said. "It'll do. But I'm starving. Let's get out of here." He took the ladder from Pablo and threw it over his shoulder. The guys could use a break.

20

The days had started to get busier. Kara set up a workspace in Green Gary's office, and that was where she stayed for most of the day. She was on the phone, mostly with bands—Do you have a drum set? Would you mind using someone else's? Can I put you in for 8:00pm? Otherwise, she was on her laptop, working on other aspects of the production. It was a state Connor hadn't really seen her in before. She would smirk at the laptop like it was telling her a joke. When she was on the phone, she'd put her elbow up on the table and balance her chin in her hand. To his credit, Gary was a hard worker as well. Since they'd received his blessing, the bookings had begun to roll in, and he was quick to take the phone from Kara when a conversation went south. He'd be in turns affable and jolly on the phone when it was needed, and then suddenly calculating and manipulative—What, the biggest concert of the year, and you can't make it? Think of the cause! I don't know if I'd be able to book you anymore if word got out that you couldn't show up for your own community! He'd taken to the activism aspect of the concert, at least for his sales pitch. It was a sort of leverage that he wasn't used to having over people.

That particular day, it was late by the time she headed back to their hotel room. He didn't mind much; he could find his own entertainment, and they saw each other each day either way. He'd been considering finding some work, maybe picking up shifts in the coffee shop his friend Steve Balboni worked at, to help fix the hole in his pocket that was his lack of employment—but he worried that the others would think he wasn't focused on the project. He'd also mentioned the idea of drumming up some new painting work on their own to Pablo and Nigel, and they'd been receptive, but distracted. Things were strange like that. He wasn't sure who had outgrown who.

Kara opened the door and set her backpack on the floor. She sat on the edge of his bed and unlaced her boots. The process always took time, since she preferred to unlace them all the way each time. She sighed as she finally squeezed one, then the other, off her feet, tossing them out of her sight. She flopped down on the bed, and crawled up, laying her head and arm on his chest, shutting her eyes. "Hey," she said. "Long day."

"You're lucky I'm still awake," Connor said, stroking her hair. He yawned.

"Don't go to sleep," she said. "I only just got here."

"You could come home earlier."

"I could. I didn't."

"You need to eat. Brush your teeth, sleep. Well, you do all those things. But you know what I mean."

"There's a lot I need to make sure happens." She sighed.

"It will happen. You've already set it into motion. And you have Gary. Gary gets things done. He'll make sure."

"I don't want it to just be his thing. We should have some say over it."

"And we do. Pablo and Nigel help out. Stirbert is doing his thing. He just has a lot of expertise. He's not a bad dude. I'm sure you've seen that by now."

"Yeah."

"I just don't want you to pour too much of yourself into this thing."

"Why?"

"What if it doesn't do what we think it will do?'

"I'm not sure if anything does what we want it to. I can't focus on that."

"I guess."

"I want to do a good job." She grabbed a fistful of his shirt in her hand.

"You do a good job. But what about after the job's done, what'll you do? Go back to painting with me?"

"You're all about the painting. You and the others."

"I'm not good for much else. I'm weird."

"It's me that's weird," she said. "People like you. They want to talk to you."

"They want to talk to you, too."

"I'm a girl, it doesn't count. They want my apple pie."

"Oh, that's gross," he laughed. "Apple pie. But it's not the worst pie I've ever had."

"Oh shut up, would you?"

They were quiet for a moment.

"Are we at the point where I can tell you things?" she asked.

"You can tell me stuff."

She picked her head up and put it on his chest. Her hand started to squeeze his bicep. "You know, I have my own issues," she said.

"That's okay."

"Sure. I guess I just thought I should tell you. Growing up I had, like, this thing with certain words, especially names. My mom, she was kind of weird about introductions. She told me that when someone introduces themself to you, you should repeat their name back at them to show that you could pronounce it. And I don't know what happened, but when I hit puberty, it was like I had to do it. Like, if I just heard a name in public, I'd have to repeat it, even just under my breath. And it got worse in high school. I would be sitting there in class, just talking to myself, and not even really realizing it or being able to help it. Just repeating every fifth word the teacher had to say. Like, 'history, president, apple,', you know, nonsense. And they would call me into the office for it, and I would start doing it to the guidance counselor, too."

"My parents didn't get it. They thought I was messing with them. They would yell at me if I did it. The worst was when they yelled my name when one of them was mad. I would just have to say it back to them, and you know, that sent them over the edge. Whatever. I'm just complaining at that point. The point is, I guess my brain got older, I went to this therapist, who was kind of okay, I guess, and I got better. I don't care about the words anymore. That part doesn't affect me."

"But I still have trouble with names. And I want you to know that. So that you can decide if you want to be with me or not. Because this whole thing, the explosion, it hurt me a lot, it's stressing me out. And it's coming back, I know it is. It's something I can control, but I can't stop it completely. It's not like an addiction. It's like there's a wrinkle very very deep inside my brain that I can't smooth out. And it just wants me to do that one thing. And there's just nothing I can do about it. I can't tell you how embarrassing it is. To not be in control. I'm sorry."

"I mean, that sounds fine to me. I mean, I'm sorry," Connor said. "I'm sorry you had to live with all that. Still have to. But I don't mind."

"It's serious," she said, looking up at him. Her eyes were red and sunken, her expression distraught. She tapped his chest once. "Go ahead, try it."

"Try what?"

"Say my name."

"Are you sure?"

"Say it," she said, tucking her hair behind each ear. "I'll show you."

"Okay," he replied, taking a deep breath. "Kara."

She grabbed his hand and squeezed, so tight that it stung. Her face reddened, and she looked deeply into his eyes. It was like she was in pain. She held her breath for a moment. "Kara," she spat out, letting her breath out, her face losing its color. She started to catch her breath.

"I'm sorry, Kara," he said.

"Kara," she whimpered back, her head on his chest. She jabbed him in the stomach with her knee.

"My bad."

He felt odd that she could trust him with something like that. Of course, he thought, he could be trusted, and he should. But it almost seemed out of character for her that she'd be willing to share. She seemed to have this sense that people didn't like or at least were suspicious of her, which was something he didn't understand. He liked her a lot. The guys seemed to think she was fun, at least. He found it confounding that he'd impressed her enough for her to stick around. Why and how he did that, he wasn't sure. He'd asked her before, and all she had little to say.

It was these moments that scared him the most. He could feel the flicker of nervousness in his chest, even as her body kept him warm. He cared about her a lot, and was smart enough to realize that, but was it good to care that much? She'd barged in the day before his life changed forever, they had a few long and short talks, and now she was falling asleep on his chest. What had they shared? He wondered if small moments like that were what intimacy actually was—not having to share much besides your presence—or if that meant they were missing something. He'd already started to feel strange when she came home later than expected. If he lost her, he wasn't sure what he'd do.

Sometimes, when they were outside together, and it was cold and the sun was down, he wanted to ask her what she really thought of him. Who it was she saw when she looked at him. He figured he could describe her perfectly if he only knew the words. He knew the way she sounded when she walked up the hotel's echoing stairwell and to their room. The way she tapped her room key on the door. The way a street light would shine in the window late at night and cast a light on her face. He knew what her nose looked like, and her eyes. How she liked to care for her hair in the morning, and where she went to get it cut. He knew the content of all that, but a description of it all was beyond him. He'd never been a person to tell a good story. Once, in middle school, he'd gotten the idea from a TV show to write a diary, and he sat and tried to describe his mother. She has brown eyes and brown hair, he remembered writing, before erasing it. Why did the color matter at all? How did that describe her? He felt like an idiot. Why couldn't he say what he really meant?

"Kara," he said, keeping his voice low, and there was no response. She had fallen asleep. Connor hadn't brushed his teeth. He always brushed his teeth, morning and night. When she was here like this, he was reluctant to move, so he pushed the urge away. He remembered a silly movie he'd watched once. The actor, some great big guy with long hair and a habit of being shirtless, said that a goat could eat anything if it had to—a goat could eat itself. The actor went on to speculate if he was just a goat in the process of eating itself. He always thought that was a bit dramatic.

21

"It's definitely a statement," Connor said, looking up at the mural, his arms folded. It was massive—he couldn't imagine how they pulled it off. He was doubly surprised when he discovered Stirbert was involved; he always assumed that he preferred the straight and narrow. He'd heard of the piece Stampy did but hadn't formed an opinion on it. This new piece was much more ambitious, and probably more subtle as an art piece than the other one, something he enjoyed. He'd also caught Pablo's signature, embedded in one corner of the mural, the same one he used on all his work – a 'P' cut into the paint with the sharp part of a trowel, with serifs added for style.

"Come on, let's take a photo," Kara said. She waved Pablo and Nigel in front of the art. They put an arm around each other and gave a thumbs up for the camera. Connor was always amused by their wide grins, the kind of smiles that only came out for photos. This was how they always did it—a brotherly embrace, and two thumbs up. It almost suggested that they were two celebrities making an appearance that was well-expected of them, contractually obligated even, but still fun. Pablo had no social media, but Nigel's was filled with photos of the various varieties of fish and chips he'd cooked or eaten, and dozens of thumbs-up photos of him and Pablo on their modest travels and exploits.

"Looks good, guys," she said. "Nice work. I'm just wondering, what's it got to do with the concert?"

Pablo and Nigel looked at each other. "I suppose the message is indirect," said Nigel. "Though the general feeling we sought to evoke... I think that feeling is in support of our cause."

"Yes, loss, tragedy, these are well-known," Pablo said. "But think of the beauty, Kara! Yes, the beauty is here, transferred onto this canvas so lovingly. You know we stayed through the night to make this? We burned the midnight oil."

He touched his hand to the dry paint, pointing out the boundaries between the abstract shapes he'd painted. "See here how the breaking of reality. We travel much like a train does, in one direction, thinking we are unstoppable. Now, we see that it all falls apart. Already, the news cameras are on their way, I'm sure!"

"I'm not so sure," Stirbert said.

The gang walked away from the mural and towards the gravelly expanse where the west end of town used to be. Pablo lifted the rope that was loosely strung around the border, and they all walked through. They rounded a small hill and a couple half-full dumpsters that had yet to be carted off and came to a flat area that had softer dirt, and less debris. A half dozen teenagers were at work below, carrying cinder blocks, rolling barrels, and carting around wheelbarrows of gravel. Green Gary was lounging on a forest-green lawn chair in the middle of all of it, directing traffic, his bifocals in sunglasses mode. He didn't shout orders, instead occasionally waving over one or two of the teenagers and explaining what he wanted, with some exaggerated hand motions. A bucket of kettle corn sat on his lap, which he devoured hungrily.

"Where'd you find these kids, eh Gary?" Pablo asked, clapping him on his back. Green Gary stood up quickly from his lawn chair, spilling a few kernels of popcorn on the ground.

"Pablo! How wonderful!" he said, reaching out for a handshake. "Yes, some local up-and-coming musicians have agreed to help us get this thing set up. In exchange for future considerations. Smart of them, I tell you! Getting that foot in the door! Bright futures are ahead of them. I just hope any of them are half-decent musicians. They're teaching a bunch of crap at the high school lately—I have half a mind to go down there and have a word with the band director about jazz theory. Come, let's do a survey."

He motioned for the others to follow. Connor had come to appreciate the swagger he always was attempting. His demeanor was that of someone aware that he could never quite escape loserdom but determined to perform swag either way.

"I've had my best man draw up some crude plans for what the place will look like. This raised area will be the stage. I'm working on a lumber connect, I think he'll come through. If he does, we will build a crude deck over the ground here, something solid to land the equipment on. If not, we'll go pick up some plywood and sort it out that way. The area around the stage, standing room only. That's easy enough, just need somewhere to stand. Off in the back and the sides, the lawn chair crowd. We found some junk around the site – barrels, logs, whatever. They can sit on those, they'll be thankful for it. Besides, there's room enough for them to set up their own chairs. I don't know why I'm so focused on chairs, I apologize. Anyways, look here—"

"What's this?" Pablo asked. A burnt-out van was being pushed over the hill. Missing its tires, the shiny metal rims rubbed against the loose rocks. The rims complained fitfully, a sickly squeal and grind, like they were embarrassed to have to move in their undressed state. It required a whole gang of teenagers to push it.

"Now this, gentlemen and lady," said Gary, "is the sound booth! Yes, we'll rig this up nicely for our sound guy. He likes to have his own space. When I saw they forgot to take this one to the crusher, I knew it had to be ours!"

"Seems like a good place to smoke," Kara said. Connor could tell she was pleased. She rocked between her left to her right foot a little.

"Well, I mean, it could use a little reupholstering," Gary replied. "But I won't stop you. Probably the sound guy will get to it before you, knowing him."

Connor peered inside the car. The leather seats were blackened with soot. The front windshield was destroyed, the glass spilled inside. The back seemed, for what it was, relatively untouched. A small knit doll hung from the rearview mirror. It was built like a totem pole, with a thick, round body, stubby arms, and two black buttons sewn on for eyes. He pulled it from the mirror and held it in his hand. It stared back at him dumbly. Hey buddy, he thought (or had he said it out loud by accident?). He put it back.

Kara took his hand in hers. "Let's get out of here. The wind's picking up."

22

Vincent Reznor was a free man. Free like a bird, he thought. Like Freebird. Free like a sample at Costco. Free like nobody was or ever could be. He'd talked his way out of another pickle, and paid precious little for it. He was starting to get his strength back thanks to his girl and his trusty vape. These were his thoughts as he had both his arms on the parallel bars at the physical therapy clinic, putting one wobbly leg in front of the other. The irony was not lost on him. His legs had betrayed him. They looked the same but didn't seem to want to work for him. The pain exhausted him, and it was with him every moment. He was getting better at walking, though, and he wanted to show Mack that he was the man. So he took one step, then another. Pain shot through his leg and through his torso, spreading cracks through his heart and his chest. He remembered what his buddy told him once, when they were high off their asses—"Like, what is pain bro, really? Next time something hurts, just think about it. Like, figure out what your body is trying to say. You'll realize that shit makes no sense." It didn't make much sense to him either. He found the spot on his calf that was bursting with pain and tried to understand it. Was it just a signal of some kind? He tried to isolate it. As he did, he realized that he'd forgotten to be hurt by the pain, if just for a moment.

"I'm here, baby," Mack said, pulling him back to reality. He collapsed into her arms at the other end of the bars, breathing in as he buried his face in her dirty hair. She'd been sweating, just from the stress of watching him work. He licked her neck, just to taste the salt. He could use a real meal.

"That's right baby. I'm so proud of you," she said. "You're doing amazing. You're getting so much better. Let's go home. You're the man, Vincent."

He tried to isolate the source of the love he also felt within him. He tried to figure out where it exactly was within his heart, his brain, or his gut. Instead of a beating throbbing pain like that in his leg, he felt only a warmth coming from his spine. It was new and difficult to master.

Days or weeks later, Vincent's strength returned, and he found walking to be less of a chore. The restaurant he cooked at had been destroyed in the inferno, but a friend of a friend had hooked him up with another gig closer to his apartment. It would be good to get back on the line. He was scheduled to start the following week. Mack had called the hospital on his behalf to see about medical bills, and they said the bill had already been paid, which was funny. The man who he'd met in the hospital hadn't come knocking again, and neither had the customs agents. He was starting to wonder if he was off the hook.

Mack opened the bedroom door, holding a sizable bouquet. "Someone's gotten me flowers!" she said, grinning widely and setting them down on the table. "I must have a secret admirer!"

Vincent laughed. "They've got an app for that now," he said.

"You shouldn't waste money on me like that," she said, leaning over the bed and kissing him. "Not until you're better and you can work."

"It was a sale," he shrugged.

"And how did you know I liked lilacs?" she asked, plucking one from the bouquet and holding it in her hand.

"I don't. They have this AI thing now. It knows everything about everyone. They even know what kind of toilet paper you like."

"Is there more than one kind of toilet paper?"

"Sure there is, baby."

"I don't know if I ever thought of it that much." She plopped down on the beanbag chair in his room and fiddled with her phone. She was a smart girl, smarter than he was, but sometimes she didn't know when he was joking about something. She wore black jeans with rough purple lilac patches sewn into the legs. She wore those pants all the time, and he liked it. It was like wherever she went, she was walking through a garden. He'd never been serious like this with a girl before, with all the belonging and longing and creepy stuff like that, so he'd been making it up as he went. He tried to remember things about her, or ask her about things he wanted to know. She was from Rochester—New Hampshire, not New York—and moved here when her parents got divorced. Her dad bet on horses for a living, and all the best races were out here, she said. She said by all measures he was a good gambler, he had an edge. That wasn't exactly how Vincent understood that gambling worked, but he figured someone had to win. He'd never met the guy.

She worked at the record store, and it was a pretty relaxed gig. She'd convinced the owner to let the patrons give her tips. She'd ring up a hundred dollar sale of a bunch of old Radiohead albums and turn the tablet to face the customer—undoubtedly some sap too old to be wearing band t-shirts or flirting with the cashier at a record store—and sometimes they'd hit '20%' tip option out of habit, like they'd just ordered a latte from a mean barista. They'd met at the record store one day, when he was picking up a Weezer record for his weed uncle. She'd turned the tablet around and smirked at him, her dumb haircut falling in her face.

"It's just gonna ask you a couple questions," she said, nodding down at the tablet, her eyes not leaving his.

He paused, noticing that they were making eye contact. "You got a name?" he asked.

She laughed. "Mack," she said, leaning against the counter with both hands, blinking. "Is there anything else I can help you with?"

It went something like that. A lot had happened since then. A lot he hadn't been able to control. But it was nice that she was there.

"Would you quit watching me?" she said, smiling.

"I'll look at you any time I like," he replied. His phone rang. He pulled it off the nightstand, and didn't recognize the number. He answered it, putting it on speakerphone and laying it on the bed where both of them could hear.

"Hello, is Vincent Reznor there?" the man on the other end of the line said. Vincent didn't quite recognize the voice. Mack put her phone down and scooted over to the edge of her bed, laying her chin on the covers and watching the phone intently.

"That's me," he said. Mack glared at him, and he gave a shrugging gesture. What else could he say?

"Vincent! Nice to hear your voice. It's your buddy, Yakub! How are you feeling today?"

"I'm doing a lot better, thanks," Vincent said. "I have my legs back. Just been trying to rest."

"That's great, that's lovely to hear. I'm ecstatic. Well, I won't keep you on the line too long. Remember when you said you'd do me a small favor? Well, it happens something came along that you can help us with. You said you can walk? You're feeling alright enough to walk around? That's good. Well, it's funny really, but there's a press conference where the governor's speaking. They're releasing the design for the park they're putting in at the cleanup site, and the new government building and ball fields and all that. We are trying to tee up a few softball interviews from the locals, to help the message get across. We'll have you sit behind the governor when she makes her speech, maybe shake her hand. Then we'll scoot you over to a couple reporters, and you'll tell them how much you like the project, you can't wait to see it all completed, things like that. Can you do that? Can you do that for me?"

Mack was frowning. "I don't like this," she whispered. "What's his problem?"

"I don't got a choice," he whispered back. Why the heck did Yakub need him for an interview? Did he look that much like a local guy?

"Yeah I mean, I guess I can do that," he said. Mack glared at him. "When's this happening?"

"Great! Tomorrow, nine in the morning," Yakub said. "I'll meet you at your place. Wear something presentable, would you? Not too presentable, of course. Be authentic."

"Can I ask why you need me for this?"

"Look, let's not go over this again. I did you a favor—you do me a favor. It's all good. I got you out of a bad situation, one you didn't deserve to be in. I'm happy to do that. But I need to do my job as well, and part of that job is stupid stuff like this. It's above your pay grade. All right? That sound good? Listen, I've got to go. Boss is breathing down my neck again, I can't just talk on the phone all day. I'm sure you have something productive to do. Be well, Vincent!"

The line went dead. "Are you crazy?" Mack said. "Interviews? What?"

"I don't know. I don't get his angle." He laid back in bed, looking at the textured ceiling of his bedroom. "Unless—hey, you're sleeping over tonight, right?" he asked.

"Yes, of course, baby," she said. "Why?"

"This is what they always do in movies—someone secretly records the bad guy admitting the bad thing they're doing, and it totally gets the good guy out of trouble. Right?"

"Yakub is a pretty bad guy."

"I don't know what he is. He seems totally off his rocker. But I think if he was trying to have me in jail I'd just be there. I guess he thinks I'm useful. Is that crazy?"

"No baby, you might be right," she said. "Okay. I'll record him tomorrow. But why interviews? I don't get it."

"I don't know. We'll just have to be ready."

"I'm sorry this is all happening," Mack said, getting into bed next to him. She crawled up next to him. "Every day it's something else with you. I just need you to get better."

He ran a hand through her hair. "Nah, I'm chilling. I still got you; it's just another day out here. Let's keep balling."

23

"No, that's vile!" Kara said. "Corned beef hash? What makes it corned? I've never heard of something so gross-sounding. You made that up."

"I'm sure you've heard of corned beef hash," said Nigel. "It's the pinnacle of American breakfast food. I name you the liar."

"No, I've never heard of that. It makes no sense. What's even in it? Is there corn?"

"I mean, look at the can," Connor said, handing her the maligned can of corned beef hash. "It's just like the picture on the can. Next time we're at the diner we can order you some."

"I'm not eating that. Besides, I said I'd eat less meat this year."

"What is less, really?" Pablo interjected. He pulled both hands from his pockets to start his verbal polemic. "Have I done less bad in the world if I eat one fewer cow this month? Has the total suffering in the world diminished?"

"People do that for health reasons as well. My buddy in England said it made him feel more energetic when he cut out beef," Nigel replied.

"I see the same girl as I have always known. Anyway, I'm being a jerk for no reason. I don't mean anything by it, you know I don't. You know there are people out there who study shrimp suffering? Apparently, we kill about 500 billion shrimp a year. That's not even a joke. And the way they do it is grotesque. I won't get too into it. That's a lot of shrimp, though. The whole thing is very confusing to me. Does a shrimp suffer less than a cow? Less than a person? Maybe the shrimp suffers only a small amount since it's got a small brain, and because we have very big, emotional brains, heartbreak is worse for us than torture is for a shrimp. But there are more shrimp than people. Ah, it's so confusing. I'm glad you're trying to reduce the suffering of cows. It's noble."

The gang had caught wind of a press conference today, wherein the governor would appear alongside the mayor, the architect, and other functionaries to reveal the plans for Nothing, the urban park. Kara had printed out some fliers for the concert to hand out to people who seemed like they'd be like-minded. Connor was privately glad that that was as far as they were planning to go—she had initially suggested picketing the event, but he argued that they didn't want to attract police attention to the event. In truth, he didn't want to have to explain his opinions on the subject to other people. The others were generally non-confrontational as well, so they were happy to go along with his line of thinking.

They'd arrived a bit early. An empty lectern sat in the middle of a road that had been dead-ended by the disaster. A series of orange traffic barrels marked the transition from road to wasteland, and a loosely hung strand of caution tape blew in the wind. A few sets of folding chairs had been set up by the barrels. A young anchorwoman sat on one of the chairs, smoking a cigarette, annoyed to be there. Some camera crews were getting set up, with middle-aged balding men tending to clusters of cables, boom mics, and satellite vans. None of these people seemed particularly enthused—the disaster was old news, and the site had been largely cleared, so there was little to see. Connor understood their thinking. Bad things happened all the time, horrible things, and those things never felt real, and he doubted it felt real to them. This one was real to him. He always got this sinking feeling when he walked through the gravel, the empty space, and the missing life and laughter. He missed his apartment and his neighbors. He missed his barber—what had happened to his barber? Had he made it out alive? He hadn't heard from him, and wouldn't know where to find the guy. He could use a haircut. There used to be shows every weekend, a basement packed full of people, music that ranged from sophomoric to life-altering, warmth, grime, and graffiti. Vines that grew long and tall over the brick facades of the buildings that turned bright orange and red in the fall. He wondered if those were the first to burn—decades of growth turned to ash and dispersed into the lower atmosphere. It was the kind of feeling he couldn't explain to a journalist. Something about how all the shrimp that lived in this particular tank of water had a good thing going, they liked their tank, even if it was dirty, and their suffering mattered, even if they were crustaceans with tiny brains that weren't made in the same image as the people that owned the tank.

"Maybe after this, we'll get into shrimp suffering," Connor said, finally breaking the silence.

"Do shrimp like concerts?" Kara asked.

"Yeah, I guess that's our only trick. That and painting. And everyone knows shrimp don't have art."

The mayor was getting ready to speak. He had a few pieces of paper on the lectern that he was flipping through idly. Connor suspected that they were not his papers. Ben, the mayor, was not one for speeches, and it was unlikely that he was about to make one now. He caught a few clips of news interviews he gave around the time of the disaster, but otherwise, he hadn't been seen much. Busy keeping things running, people would say. Some meant it charitably, some didn't.

"Is this on?" the mayor said. His glasses made his eyes look larger than life. "Am I on TV? Okay. Speaking today, we'll have the governor of the great state of New Jersey, Maura Cuomo-Romney! Thank you! Yeah, she's great, give it up. Okay, here you go, here's the mic. Enjoy, governor."

A woman with sheet metal blonde hair and dark roots stepped onto the platform and surveyed the crowd. She was younger than the average politician, but still a mother. A lesbian in a true blue state where that was a thing a girl could rightly aspire to be when she grew up. A hard worker, someone who said the right things, made the right friends, had the right parents... and here she was in the place that was kind of nowhere, giving a speech she'd given a dozen versions of before. Crisis was part of the job, but the better part of the job was what came after. Unity. Another word for the ability to write history as it was being made, and remake the present into the future.

Connor watched the governor calmly take the stack of cue cards from the podium and put them into the breast pocket of her blazer. She cleared her throat. "There's a speech written for me," she said. "I'm not going to read it. I'm tired of reading condolences. I'm sure you've received plenty of them already. If you're in need of more, feel free to stop by my office, I'm there most days. Anyway—I'd like to tell you about something I learned recently. It turns out that back in the day, before the internet, you used to have to call someone on the phone to book a plane ticket. Which makes sense, since there were no computers, but I didn't realize. I was reading this book, and this character is fleeing from the country because of some terrible crime he's committed. What does he do? He calls a travel agent, who then sets up a trip for him directly with the airline, and it's all done over the phone. It sounded like the most ridiculous thing I'd ever heard. I looked it up, and it's totally true. You couldn't just get your own plane tickets. Anyways, I'm off track, but I couldn't stop thinking about how silly that was. Things didn't always make as much sense as they do now; there was more friction. We can make things more sensible. We can smooth things over. We can build back better than things were before."

"A lot of money has flowed into this place. To be honest, I hadn't heard much from this place otherwise. It's money we'd never have been able to give you otherwise. I'm honestly excited about the prospect. Things get caught in red tape, in approvals—it's hard to spend a dime around here. We're going to get this done for you guys. It starts today. And this is where I start reading from the cue cards again. We've hired Vil, Helm & Co. to lead the design of a world-class urban park, befitting a historic gateway city to this historic metro area. A new Government Services Center, with ten thousand square feet of community space. We're going to give every teacher, police officer, and firefighter in this great city a parking spot..."

The speech kind of blew, Connor thought. People admired the governor in part because she tended to go off-script. She would always 'tell it like it is', say things just slightly beyond what she was supposed to say. In his mind, if she did say it, she obviously could get away with it. Either way, it didn't seem to work on him. He started to scan the crowd. There were a few townsfolk seated behind the governor on the stage. His eyes stopped as he saw a scruffy-looking fellow wearing a band t-shirt. Wait, was that Vincent? He knew the guy from high school. He never seemed like someone who had high aspirations in life; he was happy to smoke and flirt until the end of his days. He'd show up at a basement show now and then, looking bored, maybe with that week's girlfriend in tow. He was a cool dude.

But why was he here? Seated behind the governor, with her loyal supporters. Next to the mayor, a congressperson, and a pair of state senators. Did someone pay him off to sit there, lending a diverse character to the governor's supporters? That didn't make much sense either; the governor had always said she hated that kind of stuff, and the only thing diverse about Vincent was his relative poverty. He studied him, realizing why he didn't recognize him at first. He was gaunt, his cheeks sunken. He had more acne than usual. His eyes sat bored on his bony pale face. At the very least, he could use a nap.

Some hollering came from over the hill and around the corner. The governor paused her speech for a moment, glancing at the source of the noise, before continuing. The tone of her speech changed slightly, her voice lowering. "...including a fund reserved for families of victims. We are confident that the terms of this settlement will give lasting peace of mind for those affected. And if I could give any advice at all to those people, in this troubling time, it would be—move on. I want to build something beautiful with you, but to do that, we'll have to honor our past, yes, but also embrace the future. I'm no stranger to–"

The shouting grew louder and was accompanied by the clanging of metal. The crowd looked at one another anxiously. What could that mean? Pablo craned his neck to get a closer look, and pointed to the source of the noise. Rounding the corner were a dozen men in Roman armor. Red plumes adorned their steel helmets, and red capes draped down their backs. They carried garden equipment—spades, rakes, pitchforks. A couple of them looked positively Roman, but most of them looked like dads in a Halloween costume, their armor ill-fitting, their stomachs peeking out of the breastplate. A murmur went across the crowd. A police van rounded the corner, skidding to a stop at the edge of the crowd. A group of armored SWAT personnel spilled out, clad in black armor. They pointed their rifles at the Romans.

One of the Romans stepped forward. He was huge, at least six foot six. His armor fit him the least. "That's the guy!" Stirbert said. "He's the one who fought me."

Connor realized it was, but was too entranced by what was about to happen to care. "No longer will we be disrespected!" the man shouted, banging the handle of his rake against the pavement once. Through his helmet, which covered much of his face, only his mouth was visible, as it contorted from anger, spitting out his words. Crack. The soldiers behind him repeated the gesture. Crack.

"No longer will we be emasculated!" Crack. The cops took a step forward, jutting their rifles out at the Romans. The governor had stopped speaking and watched the scene quietly.

A loud bang went off from somewhere near the stage. "Yo, what the fuck!" a voice shouted. A firework had shot off from the stage. It exploded a hundred feet in the air in broad daylight, leaving a shower of red sparkles and smoke. The voice was Vincent's. He tossed what seemed to be a satchel of some kind off the side of the stage. As soon as it landed, fireworks began to shoot off in every direction. Some hit the sides of buildings, some flew a hundred feet in the air, and others bounced off the stage and landed on the ground before exploding, sending brilliant bursts of red, white, and blue in every direction, and a sickening amount of smoke. Someone screamed, and people started to run. They tumbled down the street, tripping over one another, as the explosions continued.

Connor felt Kara grab his hand as they left the scene. He looked back and saw Vincent being tackled by multiple armored policemen, his face pressed into the ground. He felt the world close in on him once again, as the smoke and light filled the sky and ash rained down. Was it actually just fireworks? The screams of those around him almost told him otherwise.

He let Kara tug him down the street, and he caught Pablo and Nigel following close behind. Stirbert he couldn't see. The popping and shooting of fireworks seemed to die down as they rounded the corner—there hadn't been too many people at the press conference. He tried not to choke on the taste of the air and the feeling in his gut. Kara pulled him against her chest. "It's alright," she said. "It's no big deal."

He opened his eyes and started to straighten out as he caught his breath. He looked up, and above him was the sign for the Stinky Rat, their favorite diner. He realized they'd been nearby the whole time. He took Kara's hand. Pablo kicked the door open and walked inside.

Connor looked out at the road one last time. The smoke was already clearing. What a silly little thing. He watched a Roman stumble down the street, struggling to run in the armor. He found himself hoping the soldier would get away. At least he could show that he cared about something properly. Enough to play dress up, at least. He opened the door of the diner.

24

Nigel tapped his knuckle on the counter. "Four creamers, miss," he said. "If you don't mind."

Connor sat in the booth of the diner, leaning his head against the wall. He already felt better, but Kara had her hand on his thigh, so he thought by elevating the level of anxiety he was showing she'd keep it there longer. The day was blank and bright, and the white light poured through the windows of the diner. There was something about an enclosed space with encroaching light that he loved. Something about four walls and a roof could be ecstasy. The privacy from the wind and the weather, a comfortable chair, and a milkshake.

The door of the diner swung open. Stirbert ran in, quickly shutting the door behind himself. He coughed into his fist and brushed some soot off his jacket. "Make it five," Nigel said, and the waitress agreed.

Stirbert plopped down at the booth. "Scoot over," he said, getting in on the same side as Connor and Kara. The booth could stand to be a foot larger; their bodies were pressed together trying to fit. Connor thought Stirbert didn't look himself—a bit bedraggled, really—but he probably didn't look much better himself.

"Something wasn't right about that," Stirbert said. "It's all wrong. I stayed and watched instead of running. It didn't make sense. I just couldn't believe that we were in danger."

"Fireworks are dangerous."

"Sure, but why fireworks? What's the idea there? So, say the Romans wanted to blow the governor up. Okay, then why not something more conventional? And—" he began coughing again. The milkshakes came over, and he took a hungry sip of one.

"The bag. I can't make sense of that, either. That guy. His backpack starts to blow up, why does he look so surprised? Why does he throw it away from the stage, if he's in on it? Doesn't he want it to blow up? Or did he just want to cause a scene?"

"If he wanted a scene, he got it," Kara said.

"No, the kid, he's just a local kid," Pablo said. "I know him. Connor, you know him, right? I've seen him around."

"Yes, I know him."

"He's a burnout. He has no reason to be causing that kind of trouble. What good does it do him?"

"I think he's a good guy," Connor said. "A backpack full of fireworks, though? Maybe it was some big accident. Or a misunderstanding. Maybe he had them for later."

"They're going to put him away for a while," Kara said. "I don't see a way around that."

"It's too bad," Stirbert said. "You guys think he's not with the Romans?"

"No, I don't think so," Connor answered. "It's not his style. What's he care about their politics? I don't think he could tell me who the governor was if I asked."

The waitress came by. She was the type who would seem bored of you before you even got to talking.

"The waffles, please," Connor said.

"Eh... yup," the lady said, writing it down.

"Irish bennies, for both of us," Nigel said. "Thanks, love."

The waitress rolled her eyes. "Just some cornbread," Kara said. "with butter."

"Five pancakes with chocolate chips," Stirbert said. "And a side of hash browns."

"Growing boy, Stirbert!" Pablo laughed, reaching across the table to whack him on the shoulder. "He's got wise blood in him, no doubt. This lad has continued to impress us as of late."

"So, what's this mean for the project?" Kara asked. She was always thinking about the concert. She'd started calling it 'the project', rather than a concert.

"Things might get more serious," Pablo said. "They won't take that whole mess lightly."

"They might get less serious." Connor said, and a couple people nodded. He wasn't sure what he meant by that. "Twelve dudes dressed like soldiers? A firework show? They can handle all that. That's no opposition."

"No opposition at all," Nigel said.

"We'll have something. I know we will," Kara said. "Maybe that's just the start. Sure, they're assholes, but we're not. We can get some hearts and minds on our side."

"We can only hope," Nigel said, but he didn't seem to believe her.

"The whole thing seems designed to make you feel insane," Stirbert said. "Like, just look at the place. There used to be physical places you could go and see. Real people lived there. And it's all been knocked down and flattened. I couldn't even tell you where the roads used to be, or where my apartment was, or where my favorite bench was. And everyone is saying to forget about it. Even the people who were there. Nobody could give less of a shit."

Pablo smiled as his Irish eggs benedict came to the table, along with Nigel's. The hollandaise sauce had been freshly made, a benefit to going earlier in the day. Latter-day hollandaise could be broken up and oily, but delicious still. "The milkshakes, yes?" he asked, smiling at the busser, who jogged back to the kitchen, embarrassed.

He took one bite of his hash browns and began speaking before he'd finished chewing. "The march of progress," he said. "I'm not so sure this is progress. It's like they want here to be like everywhere else. It's not a new thing. A big road, a big empty space, a big plaza. We have that. That's why people came to this free country originally, you know, the wide open spaces. But some Euros decided they'd do the whole pre-war thing and build some actual cities, some places you can walk around in. Of course, that idea has been squashed, we've buttoned up things and made sure there's no road less than six lanes wide, bless President Eisenhower in his soggy grave. But the buildings, they stay up, they're pesky like that. They preserve that way of life. It's a difficult thing, no doubt, for a planner to sit idly by and watch people walk to work, be friendly with their neighbors, and convene in public places. It is a terrible concept—to know your neighbor. The planner hates that the most. It keeps them awake at night."

"Look at us now," Nigel interrupted, a quiet signal for Pablo to stop. "Convening. Conniving. It is an utter disgrace!"

"Maybe we'll get some good music out of it," Stirbert said, as his pancakes hit the table. He plucked the top one of the pile, rolled it up into a tube, and bit half of its length at once.

"What's a fellow got to do to get a milkshake around here?" Nigel said, exasperated. He craned his neck to look into the kitchen, not seeing much besides the busy chefs. The waitress was nowhere to be found.

"How many days is it now?" Connor asked. "Until the concert."

"Six days," Kara said. She took her hand off his thigh and put it on the table. She knitted her fingers together and looked down at them.

"Does this affect our planning at all?" Connor replied.

"No, I mean... that whole thing is separate. They have their reasons, we have ours. It's great that opposition is building, though. We just can't associate with them."

"Did we get the toilets figured out?" Nigel asked. He grinned knowingly.

"Toilets? What toilets?" Pablo asked.

"Yes, it's figured out," Kara noted. "Steve Balboni had a guy. This contractor who always has some porta-potties on him. I guess he owes him a favor. He'll load them in and out on his truck."

"That's a pretty big favor," Connor said.

"But Pablo—did you take care of the thing I asked you to?"

Connor hadn't the faintest idea what Kara was talking about – but it was attractive to watch her direct traffic. "You think so little of me, Kara?" he asked. "It's done. Done yesterday."

"Pablo. Thanks. And it was done right?"

"With the utmost discretion."

Connor figured he had better not ask. Finally, the waitress came with the rest of the plates, and most importantly five creamy milkshakes.

"Oh joy," Nigel said. "Oh, my sweet cream. Come to me, love. Nigel's here for you." He took a long sip from the straw, before plucking the cherry from the maw of the whipped cream and placing it on Pablo's plate.

"Hey, suit yourself, Brit," Pablo said, flicking the cherry with his finger back at Nigel, who was too busy licking whipped cream off his fingers to care.

"What are we gonna do if the cops come?" Connor asked.

"Cops? What cops?"

"C'mon. You guys know what I mean. They'll be on edge after this. I mean, all kinds of guys. Federal. What do we do if they come to break up the event?"

"That's the risk we're taking," Kara said. "We're not doing anything wrong. Just having a concert. That's all."

"And causing a scene," Nigel said.

"Guys, it'll be fine. I swear," Kara said. She squeezed her fist open and shut a few times, pausing. "If something happens, we'll just split. We'll run. There's no fence. Just some dumb kids partying out in an abandoned place. They won't care that much."

"Nonsense, we won't run!" Pablo said. "It will be our last stand. I've always wanted a cause. I'm kidding! I'm kidding. Okay—Pablo will run away from the police."

He got some laughs for that. The conversation died down as they continued to eat. Connor's mind flew off into the distance. This time it traveled went to a memory of an educational video he'd seen in school. The teacher had been sick that day, so they'd watched a few short films the substitute had on hand. It started with a man napping on a picnic blanket. The narrator had explained that every ten seconds the camera would move ten times further away from the subject. He remembered the day he saw it first. He'd lain in bed awake that night, the dread consuming him, the narrator's voice in his head. He no longer feared it, but the waking dream still returned to him now and then.

The camera swept up and away from the diner, moving faster and faster up into the air. He saw the tops of buildings, with their fans and rooftop units, and the street grid surrounding them. Our image is at the center of the picnickers, even after they've been lost to our sight. The street grid ended abruptly at the edge of the blast radius, the network of the city coming to an end. This square is one kilometer wide, a thousand meters. The distance a racing car can travel in ten seconds. Further still, Connor saw the old city, and the new one, a gray splotch in a sea of green pastures and forests. We see the entire great city before us, in all its splendor. Ten to the fourth meters. The city vanished from view, and Earth in its entirety came into view, a blue marble against the black carpet of space.

"Connor," Nigel said, waving his hand. "You there, lad?"

"Yeah, I'm here," he said, rubbing his eyes. "Must have dozed off."

"I was asking—who'd you think could finish one of these faster? Me or greasy old Pablo? We've never had the thought to try."

"Only one way to find out, isn't there, Nigel?"

"Right-o. Waitress!"

25

An eagle flew over the prison yard and perched on the guard post. It stared at the prisoners dumbly. It was a cloudless day, the sky a bright and pale blue, the air dry. Nothing was around for miles, except this place, and the trees, the water, the fields. The first people who came to this place, with its forests and clear skies, called it the "Place where the river bends and the striped bass gathers in the spring." Those people had been killed or worse, and the river had been dammed, and now the place was called the Federal Correctional Institution at Walpack Township, New Jersey. The population outside of the prison was seven.

Vincent palmed the baseball in his state-issued glove. He'd been feeling better physically. Mentally, things weren't great. But he had to play ball. The batter, a perpetrator of a multi-billion dollar cryptocurrency scam serving twenty-five years, had a deep, swaying stance, his butt hanging close to the ground. He waved his bat wildly, his front foot grinding a hole in the dirt. Was this the best FCI Walpack had? He threw the first pitch. Slider inside, it pulls back right over the plate—but crypto guy doesn't know that. He's terrified of it. He sees the ball coming for him, and his animal instincts take over. He falls back on his rump and watches the ball sail over the plate for a strike. Jeers come from the dugout.

He gets back up, pounds his bat on the dirt, and points it at Vincent. He wasn't going to take it lightly. The guy can be angry all he wants, doesn't mean he can hit a baseball. He gave his sign to the catcher—curveball. Be ready. The catcher, a lawyer who killed his whole family by blowing up their house using a gas leak, nods, and pulls his cage down. He felt the old, chalky ball in his hand. He threw and it didn't break the way he expected. It had been a while since he'd thrown that one. It lands in the dirt before the plate, and the catcher scrambles to gather it. The crypto guy chases it, of course he does, dinging his bat off the ground. Damaging the bat like that—he should be ashamed. Vincent caught the ball. He was going to be desperate now. Why not give him what he wants? He eyed the batter. They'd all heard the stories—yachts, strippers, coke, private jets... now he was just a number. A number about to get the worst strikeout of his life.

The fastball nailed the inside corner of the plate. He had a good swing, but not good enough. He was out. He was so out that it was like he'd never been in. He should probably quit baseball entirely. Cheers came from his side, and he walked over to the gathering crowd of inmates on his team, who were pleased. High-fives and fist bumps were had all around.

"Ballgame!" the umpire shouted, waving his hands in the air. He took his mask off and tossed it in the dirt. He walked over to Vincent, and shook his hand. He was one of the friendlier prison guards and truly enjoyed the games.

"You played a classy game there, youngblood," he said. "Reminds me of how I used to be back in the day." He mocked a throwing motion.

"Thank you, sir," Vincent said. "It's been a while since I picked up a ball. Looks like I still got it."

"I'd say," the guard laughed. "Okay, like I promised. One hit of the government vape. Here you go."

Vincent took the vape in his hand. It was a forest green-colored vape, not too long, not too short. On one side "STANDARD" was printed in white block letters. He took a long draw from it, hearing it crackle. He had the urge to reach out and shake the guard. He felt his blood turn to molasses once again, in that familiar way. He fell into the gravity well of nicotine, helpless to watch the horizon fold around him. He dropped to his right knee, not in prayer, but out of weakness. It had been days, weeks maybe, since he'd had a hit like this. He handed the vape back to the prison guard, who tucked it into his shirt pocket and patted it twice.

Vincent looked at the walls and the towers around him. The cream-colored bricks were spotless—prisoners cleaned them weekly. The yard had patches of dying grass mixed with the dirt, but no debris—there were severe penalties for littering. It was a great hit, no doubt, but something about it didn't sit right with him. He looked at a scruffy man sitting in the corner of the yard—as scruffy as you can be in a place that requires you to shave your head and your face. The other prisoners said his name was Bobby. He had some cool tattoos that were mostly faded. He wasn't particularly yolked or cut like some of the other guys were. They said he even used to be a good ball player, but didn't have any will to play anymore. What was interesting, or at least notable, about him, was that he was in a constant slump of misery in the corner of the yard, when everyone else was having recreation time. They said he did it so much it gave him scoliosis. He wasn't sure if that was true.

He knew when you had a hit of a vape, a really good one, it sucked a bit of his soul out. Maybe he'd live ten fewer minutes than he was going to before. He'd always been okay with that. Nicotine would always have its place in his life. But being a federal prisoner changed that game. Did they all just end up like Bobby eventually? He remembered how Mack cared for him when he couldn't walk. How she saved him when fire rained from the sky. She was pretty metal, and she cared for him too. He felt his heart swell. She didn't deserve a Bobby. He needed to get out of here. He walked back over to the guard, who was busy laughing and joking with a couple old-timers.

"Hey, officer," he said. "Excuse me. Could you place a message for me? It won't take you a minute."

"Shit kid, maybe," he replied, taking the vape out of his mouth, and holding it between two fingers like a cigarette. "What's it for?"

"Just tell the detective I'm ready to talk."

He looked amused. "Which one?"

"You know the one."

A day later, he was sitting across from a tall man with a bushy but well-trimmed beard. He had a bony stature, and his eyes seemed to sit far back in his face. He had on a black suit with a baby blue tie and a white undershirt—and he did not look amused at all to see Vincent.

"You have a confession for me?" he asked. He had a touch of a Scottish accent, dulled with age.

"I didn't say that," Vincent replied. His lawyer made no movement. He was looking down at his papers, bored.

"So why am I here? Why make me come out here? It's a long way from the capital," he said.

"I was set up," Vincent said.

"No you weren't. Stupid kid. You tried to blow up the fucking governor. Just admit it, and I'll make sure you don't get the death penalty. Same deal I give everyone else." He clenched his fist, striking the table once.

"Easy, there," the lawyer said.

"Just listen to me for five minutes," Vincent said. "Then you can forget about me until I plead not guilty, and you get dragged back to make statements for weeks. How about that? Look, I was set up. I don't know why, but I was. I'm just a random guy. I got no intentions of blowing anyone or anything up."

"Seems like a lot of things get blown up when you're around."

"I can't help that, man. I can't help it. Look. There's this guy, Yakub. You have to find Yakub. He's the key to all of this. He's some creepy government guy. He pulls me out of prison, the last time I was there. He says I'm free and clear, I just have to do him a couple favors."

The detective took his notepad out of his breast pocket, and began writing something Vincent couldn't quite see. "Go on," he said.

"He says, come to the press conference. Sit behind the governor. Do a couple positive interviews about her whole plan, over there. That's all. Listen, I don't really care about the plan that much. I don't know much about it. I'm sure it's great. So he meets me the morning of, right? He walks me there, all normal and friendly and shit. He's giving me these instructions, he says I got to sit in a specific spot, talk to this journalist, okay, whatever. And then right when we get there his phone rings—he's all surprised and shit. Says he's gotta run after some suspect that just got out, and asks me to hold his backpack."

"So someone asked you to hold their backpack?"

"Yes sir."

"And it happened to be full of incendiary devices?"

"Fireworks, sir. I don't know shit about why."

"You didn't think to look inside it? Notice that it was heavy?"

"Listen, I'm not looking in some dude's backpack. He said he can put me in jail if he wanted to. He tells me to jump, I jump. He tells me, hold my bag, I hold the bag. I mean, can't you find this guy?"

"I mean, yeah, we'll find your accomplice," the detective laughed. He continued writing on his notepad. "I'm glad you're making it easier on us, at least. It's good to clear your conscience. We'll find him, and we'll bring him in too. In the meantime, maybe drop the whole secret agent thing. You know I don't believe you, right?"

"Why would I lie about that shit, man?" Vincent seethed. He looked into the detective's eyes, beady little ones that hated. The detective returned the stare. He'd gotten giddier over the course of the interview, laughing to himself as he wrote on his notepad.

"Everyone said you're a smart kid," the detective said. "Let me put it this way—of course you're going to lie to me. You just would. If I were you, I'd lie too. It's no sweat off my back. I actually don't hold it against you—we'll put you away either way." He had taken on the tone of a counselor, imploring him to steer his life in a straighter direction.

"You don't give a shit about the truth, do you, mister?" Vincent said. He leaned back in his chair and looked out the window of the holding cell. It was unseasonably warm outside, and unbearably hot indoors. He imagined the detective sweating through his undershirt, coming home and taking it off, throwing it in the washing machine, disgusted. That would be sweet justice.

"We might be closer to understanding each other, young man!" the detective said. He tore the front page of his notepad off and slid it across the table to

Vincent, showing him what he'd been working on this whole time. It was white lined paper, college ruled. "One last thing—I want you to see this."

Vincent reached for it. "No touching!" he said, pulling it back. "Just looking." Vincent leaned over the table to see. The detective hadn't been taking notes at all. On the paper was a crude drawing of a butt, with what seemed to be a curved penis coming out of it. The end of the penis had a smiley face.

"Well, do you like it?" the detective said. "My nephew drew this one once. To tell you the truth, I think it's art."

Vincent turned to his lawyer. "Is this shit even allowed?" he asked. The lawyer said nothing.

26

"Okay, I know it's a sound check. I'm not sure how you could 'check' what I'm doing. Are you guys familiar with my work at all?" The singer stood slouching, one hand holding a microphone, the other in her pocket. She wore an old thrifted sweater, white, with a wide orange stripe and a yellow stripe above that. Like a lazy sunset. She had wired headphones on.

"Just try," Connor said. He was standing next to her on stage, at an awkwardly far distance away. "We've been telling people, do a minute or so of your set. We just need to give the sound guy an idea of the levels he needs to set for you, and get you comfortable with the environment here. That's all."

"Fine, whatever," she said, shaking her bangs out of her face. "Fuck it. Okay, turn it on."

There was no visual response from the sound booth (the abandoned car Green Gary had sourced) but a low buzzing sound, almost like feedback, came from the speakers on stage. The woman placed the microphone back on its stand and held it with both hands. She lowered her head slightly, looking up. The noise grew louder. As it did, it was like the light left her eyes. She looked vulnerable, small. It was hard not to watch.

The tone grew louder and louder still, before splitting into a dissonant chord. A beat later, the woman screamed. She closed her eyes as she did so, using all the air in her lungs to split the air. It felt like he got punched in the chest, watching it. She screamed again, and again, and again. He felt close to tears himself. He felt terrible for her, but he didn't know why or for what. What could have hurt her that way? She was gripping the microphone, her knuckles turning white against the painted red color of her nails.

She waved her hand, signaling for the music to stop. "Did we get it?" she said into the mic, leaning into it. A thumbs-up came out of the window of the car. "Okay, great. Not sure what that was for, anyway. But I did it."

She walked over to Connor, handing the microphone over. "You alright?" he asked, and regretted opening his mouth before she had a chance to reply.

"I'm fine," she said, rolling her eyes. "Thanks." She walked off the stage. He watched her shuffle off into the gravel wasteland, back to whatever temporary housing she was living in, like him. She looked back at the stage for a moment, and he thought he saw her crying.

Connor shook the sadness away, closing his eyes and nodding his head a few times. "Next performer, please," he said, motioning towards stage left.

Walking up the gravel path to the stage was Henry Slender, the bassist for the Nopes, followed by his posse. Connor fixed the microphone to its stand. "It's great to have you here," he said, shaking Henry's hand.

"I'm glad we could come! Thanks for having us!" he said, all friendly, unlike the last time they'd met.

"I think you guys have this one covered," Connor said. "Just let me know if you need any help setting up."

"Nope, I think we got it, thanks," Henry said. His gang walked over to the assembled audio equipment and started tooling around with it.

Connor decided to give them their space and walked off the stage. Kara was waiting for him at the bottom. She embraced him and looked up at the stage.

"Busy day," was all he could think to say, kissing her on the top of her head as she watched the band set up. She'd become a real fan of the music scene in town. Half of the enjoyment she'd gotten out of this was meeting and talking to musicians. When Connor knew one of them and could introduce them, she was even more excitable.

The band started their song with a loud, friendly guitar lick. They looked like they were having fun; they were loud. They put on a good show. And then the singer, a shorter bald dude wearing a baggy sweatshirt, started to sing.

I'm not gonna do it! Nope, I won't do that! Not gonna happen! No, no, no, no!

People seemed to love their shtick. Connor was neutral on it – he wondered if they were trying to get featured on some kind of commercial, maybe for an employment law firm or something like that.

"Are you alright? You're clammy," Connor said, feeling Kara's hand between two of his.

She smiled weakly at him. "I'm fine. I just like the music. I'm tired. Not sure what it is."

"Okay, sure," Connor replied.

He paused for a moment. "Look, Gary needs—"

"No, you should help Gary. I'm okay. I'll call the performers up," she said. She looked almost red in the face. "I just get like this in the afternoon, sometimes. You know me. Go on. I'll see you later."

"Okay, sure. See you later."

He walked over to where he assumed Green Gary would be—a white canopy tent that had been pitched to the side of the main viewing area. It was enclosed on all sides except for the front, which had the flap clipped back to allow entry and exit. Inside, Gary had managed to make himself a small home. He had one of those small wood stoves you could get for camping, complete with a thin chimney that poked out the top of the tent, spewing a steady stream of smoke through the day and night. He had one of his 'assistants' (the local teenagers hoping to curry his favor) get it for him, and he'd been complaining about it incessantly. The problem, he had explained, was that he could only fit pieces of wood that were chopped relatively finely in there, and so if he took a nap or tried to spend the night, the fire was likely to go out, leaving him cold. Connor figured he would live either way.

Connor ducked inside. Gary sat upright on a comfortable couch, writing something down. One of the arms of the couch appeared to have been badly charred by fire—they'd sourced it from one of the piles of junk and debris the cleanup had produced. In the corner sat his unmistakable three-tiered cat tree—it had been carried across town, no small task. An orange cat sat at the very top of it, licking its junk. There were more comforts of home—a litter box for the cat, a small set of shelves with some of his personal effects, and papers, papers everywhere.

"Connor! Great to see you, old sport! How are things going out there?" Gary tapped his glasses, switching them to being shaded. He leaned back on the couch.

"No problems, right now," he said. "Kara is doing the lineup for me right now. I was going to ask if you needed anything else."

"Yes, I think there may be one more small thing, just one little thing you can do for me. I appreciate your initiative, here. It means a lot to me. I just need you to grab me a copy of the newspaper. You see, last week I tried to place a discreet advertisement for the concert there, and they somehow forgot to print it! It was just ridiculous on their part. A total disaster. They said they'd print it this week, this time in a bigger font. Honestly, I don't care about that little ad at this point. I mean, who even reads the newspaper anymore? It's the principle—I paid for the service, I expect to get it. Anyways—it's most certainly been delivered to my apartment unless they've managed to bungle that up too. If you could take a look there and bring it back to me, I'd be appreciative."

A walk didn't sound bad. "Sure, I'll go," he said. "But you sure you don't need something more important done?"

"I appreciate your concern, I do, Connor," he replied. The cat leaped from the cat tree and onto his lap, where he caught it, and began stroking it. "But at this stage—so close to the event—it's almost like you can't do any more preparation. You just sit back and let it happen, try not to get too nervous. You have to trust the plan."

"I guess that makes sense."

"Sure it does! Now, I've got to make a couple calls. Keep in touch! And bring me that newspaper." He reached around the cat to grab the papers that he'd been working on earlier and began to read them.

Connor eyed the stage as he left the tent. Kara was sitting on the stage, reading the list of performers. Her legs dangled off the side, slowly kicking in the breeze. An 'acoustic' act was up on the stage, a performer who seemed to only play in fits and starts, stopping a few bars in to tune his guitar, before starting over again.

The wind whipped at him, but the air was still warm. He left the gravel as he found the place where the sidewalk ended. His feet carried him through the valley of buildings, and he watched the sparse crowds of cars and people go by. He walked by the mills, and the hip coffee shop, and the river, and the hotel. A power plant spewed white smoke in the distance. The smokestack was tilted a bit to one side, but the utility company denied that there was anything wrong with it. Black birds swirled around it as it jutted out into the sky, poking above the tallest buildings and power lines.

Green Gary's apartment was a walkup, and a rolled-up newspaper sat in a green plastic bag on the stoop. Connor looked left and right, feeling suspicious. He plucked the newspaper from the stoop, stuffed it in his pocket, where it stuck out awkwardly, and began walking back. As he walked, curiosity got the better of him, and he unrolled the newspaper. On the front page sat a picture of Vincent doing his best Kubrick stare. His face was blown up to take half the page, along with the headline, 'TERROR SUSPECT ARRESTED IN FAILED PLOT TO KILL GOVERNOR'. His heart sank. Vincent was no terrorist, he knew that. But he also had no explanation for what happened. He looked at the photo again. It made him look like a thug. He was skinnier than he'd known him to be, and his stubble was growing out. He put the newspaper away. The news had already snuffed out the good mood he was in, and he didn't want to get worse. When he arrived back at Gary's tent, he heard some commotion coming from inside. He ducked in to see a girl arguing with Gary.

"Seriously, I don't know what you want me to do! This is the third time you've come and found me. I don't know how you keep doing it. You'll have to find another guy!" Gary seemed more off balance than Connor ever remembered seeing him be.

"You're the guy!" the girl said. She had a dyed red streak through her hair. "You can help me. You have to believe me. I have proof, I have a video. They did this to him. It wasn't his fault."

"Connor!" she shouted, running up to him, grabbing his arm. Now that she was turned to him, he somewhat recognized her. "Tell him about Vincent."

"Oh, are you…" he started. "Who are you?"

"Mack! Makayla! You know me. We went to high school together, asshole!" she said frantically. "Sorry. Look, you always seemed like a cool dude. Can you talk to Gary for me?"

Connor frowned. "And you know Vincent?"

"He's my boyfriend!"

"Oh. Alright. Well—I have this." He threw the newspaper onto Gary's lap, who picked it up and leafed through it.

"Interesting," Gary said. He turned the front page of the newspaper around and showed it to the group. "This is your guy?"

"Please. You have to help us," she said. "I can't lose him."

"Fine. Whatever. Clearly the world has lost its mind," he replied. He took his glasses off and rubbed his temples. "Connor, go get your girl. Put her in charge of this. I don't have the time. Or the energy." The cat meowed plaintively.

27

The parade of misfits walked out onto the gravel and towards the concert. There were the local teenagers, ears tucked into their flat brim hats. The college kids followed, cans of vodka seltzer in hand, with their girlfriends who wore high-waisted jeans. The musical burnouts were next, with their second-hand outfits and earplugs. Finally, the young professionals came, the women research coordinators with their hair pulled back, and the dude programmers in athleisure. He imagined that all those people lived around here, that they all opened their doors this morning at the same time, and walked to the show at the same time. A thousand friendly ants converging on a dropped cracker. There were people Connor recognized, lots he didn't—mostly he was relieved that anyone came at all.

People who went to festivals and concerts seemed to be good at waiting. They'd come at the listed start time of the concert, not wanting to be late. It would be an hour before the opener played. They'd do a half-hour set, and then the stagehands would set up the next act for a half hour. Finally, the show would be an hour long, maybe an encore after if the act was any good. It was a total scam. Green Gary had explained this all to them in the planning process, explaining that and said these people didn't mind being made to wait. And wait they would need to—the first act somehow couldn't find their lead singer.

Connor was leaning against a hot dog stand being run out of the back of someone's truck. A gaggle of hungry teenagers lined up, armed with twenty dollar bills. The college students were not far behind. A cheery guy in a tank top was standing in the bed of the truck, grilling twenty dogs at a time. A school bus, painted pink, had rolled onto the gravel next to the hot dog truck. How they'd gotten it there, or if they'd had permission, he had no idea. He suspected it was part of one of Gary's schemes. A lady smiled into a camera at the end of the selfie stick. She spoke rapidly about their life in the van, and the 'cute local festival' they were going to today. A bored and unsettling-looking man leaned against the bus in the background of her video, smoking a cigarette. Connor was surprised people still ripped lung darts—it was cooler to vape now.

"Hey! No outside alcohol!" Connor shouted as a college kid came in with a case of beer, with his group of friends.

"Hey man, come on," the guy said, "This shit costs money."

"I hope it does," Connor replied. "Okay, those are your friends?"

"Yes..." the guy replied. He was losing his patience quickly.

"Okay, hand each one of them a beer," Connor said. The college kid did as he was told. "Now, everyone crack open the beer."

They did so, looking at him, confused. "Okay, you're good to go," Connor said, laughing to himself. The kids kept moving, swearing to themselves. One chugged their beer right away, and threw the crushed can on the ground. Connor walked over to pick it up and stuffed it in his pocket, watching the college kids recede into the growing crowd of music fans.

"Hey, my friend! How are you?" The voice belonged to Pablo, walking up to him. He gave Connor a big hug with one arm, his other hand holding a trash bag. "The day is finally upon us! Who knew rebellion would be so easy? Everyone just shows up to the event at the listed time!"

"We're changing the world," Connor laughed.

"Oh, I'll take that!" he said, taking the can out of Connor's pocket, putting it into his trash bag.

"Where'd you find that stupid shirt?" Connor said. "You look ridiculous."

"Oh, this?" Pablo started. It was a neon orange T-shirt that seemed to be a size too small for him. It made his already large frame look even larger. "Me and Nige wanted to have shirts that said 'STAFF' on them. This was all we could find at the thrift store."

He turned around and pointed his thumb at the back. In blocky font, it read 'CARNIVAL STAFF'. "Carnival? You serious man?" he laughed.

Pablo turned his nose upward. "My only regret is that I could not get one for the rest of you! Anyways—I'm not here just to give you a fashion show. I wanted to ask you something. The girl—Makayla, she wants to make her presentation, like we discussed. But it turns out, the singer from the band that's about to come up—I think they're called the Drunk Skunks or something like that—he needs to sober up before he can play. So we're just going to let her do it now. And you were the one who set up all the HDMI cables and stuff like that last time for the projector for the rehearsal, and they're trying to figure it out over there, but something's not working. So if you could just run over there, maybe, then that would be great."

Connor nodded and headed over to the sound booth. The rusty car had a projector strapped on top. It looked like WALL-E. A gas generator hummed in the distance, providing what meager power they needed for the show. How Gary had gotten a generator, he had no idea. Inside the car, Makayla was arguing with the audio technician.

"I don't understand! It worked perfectly yesterday. Don't you know where it goes?"

"I told you," the man explained, exasperated. "I'm audio-only. No video. I'm not even getting paid!"

"Okay, okay, let's see..." Connor said. "Hey, Mack. How are ya, how ya been? Okay. Let's take a look."

He spotted the problem immediately. Somehow the video cable had been plugged into the projector, looped through the car, and plugged back into the projector. That wouldn't work. He made the fix quickly, and the projector came to life, projecting a blue screen on a large bed sheet that had been strung up behind the stage on the last day—Kara's idea.

"Okay, I'm sorry. Thank you," Mack said. She leaned over the laptop and opened the video file she wanted to play. "And the audio is on?"

"Yes, it's on."

"Okay, amazing," she replied, hitting play. Connor ducked outside the sound booth.

The sun had started to move in the sky behind the stage, bathing the gravel lot before it in white light. An array of microphones, amplifiers, and other equipment sat unused on the stage. The screen started with static, before cutting to black with white text. The text read: DO YOU KNOW THIS MAN? The crowd seemed to be paying it a small amount of attention, more focused on getting hot dogs or crushing beers to notice. Some guests had gathered on one side of the pit to smoke, and a small plume was rising from their gathered mouths.

The video switched to footage of a bedroom with three people inside it. The camera was set up on a nearby surface, probably a desk. The occupants of the room didn't seem to be aware of it. Mack was laid up on the bed, looking bored. Vincent, he recognized, stood next to the bed, hands in his pockets. By the door was a third man—wearing a light brown trench coat, and no hat. He had a smirk on his face as he spoke. He had a bulky black backpack on him, and it seemed to be quite full. Everyone knew that one didn't wear a nice coat with a backpack; you needed a satchel of some kind or a briefcase. The crowd was starting to get more interested—the conversation on the screen wasn't terribly interesting, just some small talk—but the faded grain of the projector gave the strange man in the coat an alluring noir vibe. Watching a video was always more interesting than talking to your friends, so people started to cease talking and looked at the screen.

The film cut to the title card again—DO YOU KNOW THIS MAN?—and switched to handheld footage. It followed Vincent and the man at a distance, as they walked down the street. The person filming, presumably Mack, would periodically duck behind a bush or a trash can, and zoom in, showing the audience what they were doing. A cheer went up from the crowd as this happened—the missing band had started taking the stage. The lead singer, still roaring drunk it seemed, stumbled up to the microphone, and then threw up off the front of the stage, which only resulted in more cheers from the crowd. From him, they expected and adored it. He heard swears coming from the audio booth—Mack, probably. But there was nothing they could do to stop the band from starting. They were already running late.

The video continued to follow Vincent and the man before it reached an area relatively close to the new 'edge' of town. The man in the trench coat stopped, and took a phone call. It seemed urgent. The camera was too far away to capture audio. He handed the backpack to Vincent, and pointed down the road, giving hurried instructions. He then dashed away down a side street, leaving Vincent carrying the heavy backpack. The band started to play. Heavy guitars clashed with one another, the kind of tones so deep and distorted that the crowd would probably be looking up the chords online afterward. The singer started almost right away, his voice a full-throated wail. It didn't seem like English—might be Korean. The camera zoomed in on Vincent. He stared at the black backpack in his hand for a moment. Did he know, in that moment, what was about to happen? Did he feel ice crawl up his spine? Was it cold that day? He shrugged and put the backpack on.

It cut to the title card again, before picking up footage, not of Vincent, but of the man in the trench coat. It followed him walking at a leisurely pace down the street – clearly not in a hurry, or answering an urgent phone call. There was a skip in his step. The band continued in a crescendo, pushing the meager speakers they'd sourced for the event to their limits. The crowd was nodding their heads with great fervor. Some people around the front were starting to push on the railing in front of the stage, as if this were a real concert, with security guarding the stage. There was no security. The man ducked into a cafe and sat by the window. The camera panned away from him for a moment, as it found a convenient bench across the street. Mack crouched behind it and pointed the camera at the man.

There was little glare on the window of the cafe, but you could see the man sit and check his phone. There was a bar with three stools and a bored-looking barista wearing a flat brim hat. Pleasant globe lights hung from the ceiling, giving the interior a warm amber look. As the man sat, he reached one hand down the back of his pants and scratched his butt. He pulled the hand back out and sniffed it. The crowd cheered more, as the music continued, the guitarist taking a vengeful solo. The barista approached the man, laying a coffee on the small square table he sat before. As she departed, he groped her. She whipped around and socked him in the eye, seemingly to his surprise. A roar came from the crowd, enraged at the man's behavior. This was definitely something they did not condone.

The man in the trench coat stumbled out of the cafe, holding his warm coffee cup to his eye. The title card showed again, and it cut to him in a crowded bar. How she managed the angle she had of him, he couldn't imagine. He was leaning against the bar, staring down a Kahlua shooter, black eye showing. Passersby occasionally blocked the camera as he drank. Two women were at the bar next to him, barely listening. He said something inaudible to the bartender, who brought two shots to the women. Connor thought they might have been green tea shots. Suddenly, the tone of their conversation changed, and the man stood up angrily, shouting at the women. A burly man in a black t-shirt quickly hauled him outside, picking him up by the armpits. They said some choice words to each other as they exited the bar, but the man left without protest until his stomach suddenly lurched. The camera followed him, catching the moment his coffee-colored vomit glazed the already filthy window of the dive.

He laid against a lamp post, sinking to the ground, his face wan and broken, but pleased. The delight of a man at the very bottom, his butt to the earth, sitting splayed like a baby. Mack snuck up behind him, positioning the camera to point at his glowing phone. It took a moment for her to focus it on the screen. He ordered a car, and then flipped to a betting app. His parlays were failing—he'd bet on the coin toss of the Eagles game to land on the rim of the coin, neither heads nor tails. He thought he had it at +50,000, but the coin landed on heads. He closed the app and hung his head. Mack must have moved behind him, as he whipped his head around quickly. The band's song was winding down, into a still-loud diminuendo of guitar, bass, and drum arguing together. The crowd was thoroughly entertained, rocking to the music, stimulated by the video. Everyone from the teens to the young professionals watched intently.

"Hey, you! Are you following me? the man in the trench coat shouted, drunk. "That won't do anything. You're powerless in this situation. It's already done! Don't you watch the news? He's going to jail! For a long, long time! And you'll be there with him too!"

As he reached for the camera, the video froze on his twisted, cruel expression. The veins in his forehead, the hate in his eyes. It faded to black, to raucous cheers from the crowd. The ending of the video was a series of black and white documentary-style captioned images: Vincent's high school senior photo, him smiling, looking cleaned up. 'Vincent Reznor has been framed', it wrote. It switched to a photo of the man in the coat, looking sad at the bar. 'This man is responsible, it said. 'His name is Yakub'. The name Yakub turned red, and the video faded to black. The sophistication was a bit shocking.

The band shuffled off stage, and the video minimized, showing the computer desktop. The background was a pleasant AI-generated photograph of a litter of puppies. The projector switched off, and the crowd talked amongst themselves excitedly. The word 'avant-garde' was being thrown around. The next act on stage was the beautiful screaming girl. Connor saw it as a success—they'd gotten a lot of eyes on the video—but if that mattered, he couldn't say. He decided to go backstage and see if Kara needed any help. A flock of seagulls flew West, in their daily migration to the dump. And the woman on the stage started to scream.

28

The day had grown long. The hot dog stand had run out of dogs, and its owner packed up and left. The RV dwellers had gone back to their RV and shut the curtains. The crowd was still strong, but starting to tire. Connor didn't want to imagine the state the porta-potties were in. He'd found out today that Kara called them 'Porta-Johns', a name he found inexplicably offensive. The green room, as it were, was an assortment of old couches and tables scattered behind the stage that had been soaked with rain and sun-dried a dozen times, aging them. They were lucky to have a few days of dry weather before the concert, as it meant the couches were still usable. Connor sat with Kara on one, his arm around her.

She tugged on his shirt. "I don't mind this," she said.

"I'm glad you think so."

There was not much else to say. The last band was getting ready to go on stage, a group of shaggy people from Philadelphia. They were a great band, everyone knew, and their being not heinously attractive made their appeal better. Workmanlike people that you might see on the street. The female lead sat on a stool, grimacing at her guitar as she tuned it a full step down. She hadn't acknowledged him and Kara at all.

"Do you know them?" Kara asked.

"Yeah, I've met the bassist once." At least he was pretty sure he had.

She smiled at that. Things had, in general, gone well. The concert was not without its hiccups—drunk acts, no-shows—but those were things they planned for. The crowd had been well-behaved. They hadn't heard a peep from the police department, though that may have been Gary's doing. Kara was exhausted but seemed to be in good spirits. She certainly had put in the work. She seemed to relish long days. Her favorite days with him were when things started in the afternoon and stretched long into the evening, an evening out turning into a quiet sleepless night, fighting sleep at three in the morning, him looking up at her, never down. She told him the first time he fell asleep while they were together she had been surprised. She had looked over and he was asleep. Soon it would be ten in the morning, and she'd be looking for a coffee which he'd buy and she'd insist on paying him back for. After those nights, it always was a surprise that she would be there in the morning. The late nights were hard to remember and hard to describe—it was more warmth and fuzz than it was a real thing you could pin a memory to. The morning was when he was at his most energetic and intellectual, and it was the opposite for her. Their signal to get up those days would be him rolling her sleeping body off of his, so he could go use the bathroom. He would usually come back from the bathroom to find her awake, looking back at him a confused expression on her face. Her hair inevitably messed up. He could never tell, in the end, how someone was actually feeling. The eyes could only say so much.

He realized that while his waking dream was happening, she'd fallen asleep. It was unlike her to do that. The band had started to play. The lead singer dancing along to the beat, riding the groove of the moment.

"You look like a telephone pole leaning over—" she sang in a friendly alto voice. "—I remember that the most when it rains back in Dover."

A half hour later, the band was done, and the crowd was starting to shuffle out. Connor rolled Kara off of him, and walked over to the stage. He found Stirbert standing by the microphone, as the band packed up their guitars and other equipment. He had a wrinkled piece of notebook paper in his hand. Stirbert stepped up to the microphone, looking down scared at it for a moment, almost as if it were a device capable of hurting him. Connor waved at the sound booth quickly, hoping someone would turn the microphone on.

Stirbert looked down at the paper and back out at the crowd. "Hey everyone," he said. His shaky voice was amplified over the quiet rabble of the people who were starting to head out.

"I'd like to thank everyone that came out here today. My name is Stirbert. I'm one of the people who helped put this whole thing on."

A polite cheer came from the crowd. "A lot of hardworking, amazing people helped do this, and I'm sure they don't want me, uh, reading their names to you. So I won't do that—but they know who they are. We also had so many amazing bands come out here today, and you know, we didn't have money to pay any of them. They did this for our community."

"I know a few different bands touched on this during their sets, but I just wanted to you know, close this out by reminding you guys why we are all here today. I don't know what neighborhoods you guys are from—but we lost a lot. We lost everything we had. I think my friend Connor lived not far from where I'm standing. You'd never know that, walking around here. It's all gravel now. You know, maybe he had to lose his apartment, maybe he didn't. But, like a lot of the people that performed here today for you, he has nowhere to go. In a few days, the hotel they're paying for will kick him out, and he'll have to move. I'm sure, you know, he'll be fine—he has a good support system—but a lot of us won't be. A lot of the musicians you saw here today."

He folded up the paper and put it in his pocket. Connor wanted to sink backstage, to not be visible in that moment, but he found himself unable to move. "I think a lot of us assumed, originally, we'd get something back. There's a reason this place had so many good bands come out of it. It was a really vibrant place, a place where you could, you know, have a band or make art and pay your way with very little. We all kinda lived on top of each other—you could walk down the street and you had everything you needed right there. Groceries, coffee, beer, you know, whatever floats your boat. And that's all disappeared. And I don't really understand why, but it's like nobody cares. The people in charge, you might know that they want there to be nothing there to replace it. They want parking lots and open fields and empty space. They want wide open roads with turning lanes and traffic lights and predictable layouts. They hate us and our lifestyle. I'm not smart enough to say why. I think, if you ask me, we had a pretty good thing going. Hopefully the music is a testament to that. So, I guess I'm rambling at this point—but if any of that matters to you at all, speak up. Do something about it. We're out of time at this point. I hope you enjoyed the music. I love that we got to share it with you. Okay, I'll stop talking now. Can someone shut this mic off? Thanks."

What remained of the crowd applauded. What they really thought, it was hard to know. Connor lurched forward, finding Stirbert leaning against the microphone stand.

"Hey man," he said, drawing him in for a hug. Stirbert buried his head in Connor's shoulder and hugged him back. "You did a good job. You did the right thing. That was great."

He put his arm around him and walked him backstage. Kara was awake, and wiping a tear from one eye. She hugged him as well. "Thank you," she said, her voice shaking.

An eternity later, the five painters walked in a line down the gravel field, trash bags in one hand, grabbers in the other hand. Connor picked up a Michelob Ultra from the ground and placed it in the bag. "One hundred three," he said.

They cleared the ground systematically, freeing the Earth of aluminum cans, hats, water bottles, paper plates, discarded hot dog buns, and wads of gum. Pablo showed them his latest find—an unopened condom, which he waved in Stirbert's face. "Saddest story ever," he said. "For Sale: Condom Wrapper, never opened."

"I could weep," Nigel said, picking up the guts of a burrito whose contents had spilled onto the ground.

Green Gary was nearby, watching two teenagers fold up his tent, giving instructions as they went. Already his personal effects and furniture had been removed. The toilets were being carted off in a truck. Some other people were rolling away the old logs and barrels that had been used for seating. A group of people were boxing up what remained of the stage.

"To think," Pablo said, "soon it will be as if nothing happened!"

"I'm starting to think that things always have happened, and cannot be undone," Nigel said, "or perhaps that's just what I need to believe to keep going on."

29

The Scot detective cut his stare into an array of microphones and cameras before him. His eyes hated, in the way many eyes did. He was probably longing for whiskey.

"Has the FBI reviewed the new footage?" a reporter shouted over the fray.

"We are taking all leads into account."

"There's a viral claim that Vincent Reznor was framed; is he still your primary suspect?" another asked.

"I can't comment on that. He's the subject of an active investigation."

"Who is the man in the video?"

"He's a person of interest. If anyone has information on this 'Yakub' character, they are encouraged to come forward."

Mack heard a knock on her front door and switched the TV off hurriedly. The detective blinked off the screen and was replaced with a black mirror. She threw a mostly-finished can of Boom into the trash, and wiped the crumbs off her sweater.

"FBI," a disinterested voice spoke from the other side of the door.

She sighed and opened up. The agent didn't even bother to speak—he just grabbed her upper arm and led her away. She was happy to come with him. Things were finally looking up.

"Who the fuck is Yakub?" the detective said, throwing a binder across the room. The word fuck was mangled by the way he spoke, adding a guttural, hacking quality to the expletive. The binder hit the wall, and the pages it contained scattered across the floor. Mack glanced to the ground and saw several printed stills from the video. He removed a toothpick from his pocket and placed it in his mouth, sucking it hungrily.

"I don't know Yakub," she said. "That's the truth."

"Yeah, well you knew him enough to make that little fan film of him. Nice work by the way—you have completely taken the piss out of this investigation. You could have just sent it to us. We'd have looked at it already." The lines of stress showed on his forehead.

"Nobody ever listens to me," she said. "It's the same thing every time. From him and from you. I don't believe you, I know you did it. Nobody listens! I'm so fucking done with that. I'm not interested in having that conversation anymore."

"Okay," the detective said. He flipped his chair backward and sat, his chest pressed against the back of the chair. His hot breath hit her as he spoke, and her eyes burrowed into his. "Say I believe you. Say I already know who Yakub is, but I can't put the pieces together. And, like it or not, I can't let the guy who was holding a fucking bomb walk free when I don't have my fingers on someone else."

"Why would you believe me?" Mack said, shrinking back in her chair to escape him. "What's changed?"

"Cause it makes no fucking sense!" the detective shouted, standing up again. "Your boyfriend, nice kid by the way, he's a moron. All he does is ask for his vape and yap about this Yakub creep. He's not smart enough to invent all that on his own. Plus—the video checks out. Oh, the video. The stupid video."

"What's wrong with the video?"

The detective removed an old-fashioned tape recorder from under the table and placed it between him and Mack. He pressed the play button.

"Hey, uh, this is Cindy, I work at the dollar store," a voice came from the tape. The tapes span steadily in the machine. "I think I know the guy in the video. He comes into the store here to buy scratch-offs. I mean like, loads of guys do that. But he always makes some gross comment to me. He's the worst. Maybe you'll catch him if you send an officer here. I don't know if that helps or anything. Bye!"

The detective didn't seem amused. He pushed another button on the tape recorder.

"This is Blake. I'm a trash man," said the man on the tape. He had a kind and aged voice. "My daughter made me come out to this concert, and you know, it's white people music, for sure, this Junk stuff. It's not something I'd listen to—but she likes it, so I'm there."

"The band played that video of the dude Yakub, and then I was scrolling and I saw his face getting posted on the news, and I thought, well, Blake, you gotta call this in. Because y'know, when you go out on your route, picking up trash every day, you see a lot of the same people. A lot of the same faces. That's my community. I'm happy to serve them. One day, I'm pulling a double shift, and this guy is puking in one of my trash cans. That's fine with me. But this dude ain't wearing any pants! I go to take the trash can away, and his hog is just hanging out. Then he called me—"

The detective hit the 'off' button on the tape recorder, cutting the man's voice off. "First of all," he said. "We have a suspect who claims to be some kind of government employee, but there's no trace of him on any database anywhere. Facial recognition pulled up someone named Brian, who died in a training accident in the Marines ten years ago. Not a trace of that name anywhere besides the obituary. Second of all, everyone's apparently been seeing him around town lately, and nobody's thought to speak up. Not a word until now! We could have taken him in for beating it in public, but the local garbage man didn't think that was important. And third, he's fucking canceled! They canceled him! What's the point of that? They cancel my fucking suspect! What does that even do? He's already a criminal. He doesn't need to be canceled. He has more allegations than a standup comedian."

"They have this guy on the news!" he said. "His face is on the news."

Mack laid back in the chair and watched him sputter, and then leaned forward. "Why," she said, "is that my fucking problem?"

"It's not. I don't give a shit. I can keep your boyfriend as long as I want," the detective said. He ran a hand through his brown hair. "But I don't think he's the guy. He's not the guy. He sure did it, he sure made that little fireworks show, but I don't think he meant to. So—I'll get to the point: Is there anything you haven't told me? Anything that could help me find Yakub?"

Mack stretched her arms out over the interrogation table and looked down. Her hair fell over her face. What kind of girl had she become? Mixed up with the law over a man? She always wondered if young Makayla would be proud of who she was today—if she was letting that girl down. She didn't think she was.

"Don't you think he's gone? Like, long gone?" Mack asked. "He seems like a pest and a drunk, but I talked to Vincent. He is one hundred percent sure that this guy is some kind of spook, like you, no offense. And he had the power to get him out of other kinds of trouble. And then he stages some kind of hokey terrorist attack with like, a non-lethal weapon? He's smart enough to just leave. He's probably back in Virginia having a cigar. He's laughing at us right now, arguing over who gets custody of my gullible idiot boyfriend. It don't got shit to do with me or you! If you ask me, that dude was playing God, that's all."

The detective put his head into his hands. "It's all so fucked," he said.

"No, you did a great job," Mack said. "You were really scary. And I'm just a girl—you know, I work at a record store. I don't have a degree. You had me ready to confess to anything, I mean it."

"Shut up, would you?" the detective laughed. "I can't believe I'm doing this. Okay, you can have your boyfriend. You can take him home with you if you like. Just tell him to lay low. No skateboarding, eh? That would do him some good."

Mack had to stop herself from leaping to her feet and hugging the man. Instead, she grinned widely and reached out for a handshake. "Pleasure doing business with you, sir," she said.

30

The city councilman glanced down at his notepad and back up at the audience. He wore a yellow striped shirt and a dark blue tie. A pen was tucked into his breast pocket. His hair was darker than it should have been for a man of his age, darker than the gray walls of the council chamber.

"We have eighty people signed up to speak tonight," he said. "That means that we have to limit everyone who comes up to the microphone to just one minute. After the public comment period is over, we're going to vote on the measure. I'm going to predict in advance that all the other business will have to be taken care of at the meeting two weeks from now. Okay, we'll begin. This meeting is being broadcasted right now, so if you come to speak, you do consent to being recorded. Okay, thank you."

The councilor shuffled papers on his desk as the first speaker, an older woman, came to the microphone. "My name is Patricia, I live at 100 Brattle St," she said, leaning into the wooden lectern. "I support the project. My dentist used to be in the west end of town, and it was so hard for me to find parking. I usually would park at the grocery store and walk a few blocks to get to him, and the entire time I felt unsafe—the narrow streets, the vagrants and the teenagers walking around, it was all too much. Open space, green space, you know, that is what we need to be resilient as a city. That's climate justice to me. Thank you."

Some clapping came from the crowd. Next in line was an older gentleman in a blazer. "Hey friends, I'm Peter, I'm a professor at the community college. I live at 301 Fulkerson Street. You know, I love the sun. My zucchini garden happens to be down the road from this place. And it really broke my heart when this whole disaster happened. But we put things back together, like a community. And I noticed when I walked outside today—at four o'clock, my zucchini garden was getting some late afternoon light it didn't before. I've always loved the sun: it strengthens us, it gives us life and happiness. Tall buildings, apartments, they block the sun. They cleave us apart from one another, believe it or not. So I implore the council to vote 'yes' on this measure, as a yes to more sunlight, and more zucchini. Thank you!"

Connor's heart sank. Where had these people come from? Didn't they know anything? The next person up to the lectern was a middle-aged man with a mole on his left cheek growing a single long hair.

"I just can't believe what I'm hearing," the man said. He wiped a tear from his right cheek. "They are putting feminizing chemicals in the water! And we're all just happy to go along with it. Or maybe, that's what you all want. You want to destroy our young boys and girls with this nonsense. The liberal professor, the liberal crone! What kindly people to steal our freedom and our traditions away from us! You—"

"Okay, I'm cutting the microphone," a councilwoman said. Connor recognized her as Councilor Cringlesworth, who he'd met ages ago. "For everyone's reference, you know we can't say things like that. Let's keep the focus on the project. And—if I can be frank here, after the attack on our brave governor, I think the other councilors and I will have a very low tolerance for remarks that impugn this project in such a manner. Hate has no home in this place in this free country. Okay, next speaker, please."

The next person up was someone Connor recognized—the female singer who had screamed so loudly at the sound check. She was wearing a long sweater and ripped jeans. "Hey there, I'm Carla," she said. "I used to live at 10 Buick Street in the west end of town. Now I live at the Holiday Inn and Suites across from

Chili's, or I will for the next few days. I just wanted to say, maybe in case it wasn't obvious, that I loved my neighborhood. I loved living there. I met all my friends and my bandmates there, they're who helped me succeed and be who I am today. And I just can't believe that nobody likes us or wants to stand up for us. I have totally nowhere to go. I'll have to leave, I think, to live with my aunt in Boulder. I thought at least there'd be some focus on rebuilding things—but it seems like you guys want anything but. So I'll have to oppose the project. Thank you."

Applause came from the younger people in the room. The next speaker was a member of her band. "I'm Dave," he started. "I play bass. I used to live at 10 Silber Way, but now I live at my girlfriend's mom's house the next town over. She's kind of a handful to deal with. Anyway, I oppose the project. We deserve to get our community back. I don't understand what you're proposing to replace it with—empty space? We have plenty of empty space. The real empty space is the rest of the city, all that sprawl and food chains and crud like that."

Hissing came from the crowd. Connor hated the hissing. As a gesture, it felt very inhuman.

Dave waved his hand at the audience to quiet them and spoke into the mic again. "No, really. I mean it. You guys live in houses that are eighty feet apart. You don't have to hear or even talk to your neighbors. You don't wear rain jackets because you never feel the weather. That's not how I want to live. I'm sorry, but it's not. I don't get why you want to force that on everyone else. I thought this was a free country, after all."

More hissing from the crowd. Dave went back to the pews and sat down. Kara was sitting next to him, holding his hand tightly. They hadn't said a word to each other since the meeting started. Pablo was next in line to speak.

He stretched his arms out wide and beamed at the city council. "Friends, neighbors, comrades. We stand at the precipice. The decision you make today will have generational consequences. I stand before you humbled, the last representative of a dying culture and way of life. Nobody will remember the tragedy that happened that day as your fault. However, the tragedy you choose to inflict again today, that is the one that will be remembered. Children will open a history book and see photographs of our smiling faces, our way of life, and ask where it all went. And the next page will list your names and the reasons for which you voted today to remove us from the community. And you'll be on the wrong side of that history."

"Doesn't anyone love beautiful things anymore? We have all the beauty we need here, it is gathered around you. Yes, the fire came. You can pull beautiful things from the fire. If in your life you can only save one thing, let this be it. Let the west side of town be it. It would be a life well lived."

"That's all the time allotted, sir," a councilor said. Silence filled the room. "Thanks for your comments. Next speaker, please."

The meeting continued in that fashion, those opposed and those in favor saying their peace, things at times getting out of hand and having to be quelled by the steady voice of the councilman. It took an hour and a half of sitting to get through it. His butt grew sore, then numb, then sore again. About a third of the people who went up left after speaking. In a way, Connor had already prepared himself for either outcome. He'd grieved all day over it, his stomach aching and his nails chewed.

Kara was not in much better shape. She looked pale, and her hands felt clammy. Her sadness revealed a different character about her. He still found her beautiful, but her face was sad, her hair slick and almost greasy. She wore a cardigan and slacks to the meeting, which was unlike her. It was like a different woman had turned up to the city council meeting. He put his hand on her thigh, just to see if she was still his, and she let him.

"That concludes our public comment period," the councilman said. "Thank you to everyone who showed up and made their voices heard. Now, for the next part of the process, I'll turn it over to the mayor to give his thoughts on the matter."

"Thank you," Mayor Ben said, adjusting his glasses. "I want to draw attention to the fact that this is a delicate matter. I appreciate the many voices that came out here to speak today. I know this isn't an easy thing. I hear you, and I see you. I know I don't get out in front of you all saying this enough, so I'm saying that today. I usually see a dozen or so people at a meeting like this, and we probably hit a hundred today. That tells me we need to consider this carefully."

He cleared his throat. "Luckily, we have been working very hard on this. A lot of funding has come our way, and we have to get it right. I think the housing support and the relocation terms that have been offered to those affected have been very generous—but they do cost money. I can't balance the books while giving everyone a free ride. I just think, you know, someone said tonight that this is a generational event. I see it as a generational opportunity. I think this is a case where we have a chance to set this town up for the long-term future, as we put the pieces back together. So that, in sum, is why I'm voting for the proposal."

"Now, I'll ask the city council if they are ready to vote. Does anyone object to starting the vote?"

Nobody moved.

"Okay, I'll open this up to voting. I'm registering my vote, that's an 'aye'. Councilor Cringlesworth, please take your feet off the table."

"Sorry, Ben," she said, dropping her heels to the ground with a clomp. "Aye."

"Councilor Schraeder?" the mayor asked.

"Aye."

"Councilor Slohoda?"

"Aye."

"Councilor Baker?"

"Aye."

"Councilor White?"

"Aye."

"Councilor O'Brien?"

The very last person seated at the table was a man of about forty. He was short, with round glasses and a round face. He frowned at the audience, and then at the other councilors. "Nay," he said.

"That is six to one, the motion is passed and this meeting is adjourned," the mayor banged his gavel and swiftly walked out the back door of the room. A hush flew across the room.

Pablo was the first to stand up. "Into the dustbin of history we go," he said. "Gentlemen, lady. We should go have a drink. Let's leave this miserable place."

Connor looked up at him. He couldn't think of anything he wanted less than a beer right now. Kara didn't seem like much in the mood either—she was holding herself and staring at the floor.

"It's okay," he whispered to her, putting his arm around her shoulders. "We did everything we could."

Was there something he could have done?

Nigel nodded. "I'm dreadfully sorry," he said. He followed Pablo out of city hall. Stirbert was nowhere to be found.

Connor sat with her for a while. He imagined that he was at the very bottom of the Earth, the South Pole. An icy tundra, the wind swirling around him, white snow blowing steadily across the flat expanse. An impossible, great hand reached out from the universe beyond and grasped the globe in its fist. It shook the Earth once, setting him free of its gravitational pull, flying forever downwards, out into space, a place even colder than where he'd been before. When he came to his senses again, Kara had slipped away.

31

H e was lucky he had so few possessions. He threw the books, the clothes, the cords, and the keyboard into boxes. Kara had already packed her things and stripped her bed, leaving just a stack of dirty sheets, six boxes, and a backpack as her artifacts. As he finished his work, he sat on the empty mattress and stared at the wall before him. The hotel art across from his bed was a photograph of a window set into a brick wall. The entire image was recolored to be a baby blue. Through the window was a cream color, as if the building were brimming with it. Connor would look at the image sometimes. He had no idea what the artist had meant by it. Maybe they didn't mean much at all, and that was why the art was in a hotel and not a gallery.

Kara let herself in, the door creaking as it slowly shut itself behind her. She had her hair up in a clip. It was unusual for her—it made her look French.

"Hey, Connor," she said. "My friend is going to pick up my stuff in her truck in like an hour. I gave her the extra room key."

"Oh, great," Connor said. "That's easy, then. I think you'll like the guest room at Steve Balboni's house. It's weirdly high up, you kind of have to jump to get on it. But after you get used to it, you kinda look forward to the jump. It's a funny thing."

She looked at him and smiled. So little that it was barely a smile at all. She sat on the single office chair the hotel had provided, and swung left and right.

"You know, if we have an hour, we could get pizza downstairs. Unpacking could take a while, we'll be hungry if we don't eat."

It was an awkward position. Him lying in the unmade bed, and her in the chair. It forced her to look down at him. Her eyes looked glossy. She hadn't taken her shoes off.

"We should probably say goodbye to the guy who runs the shop across the street, too. He'll miss us, I think. Do you think he'll miss us? He's such a nice guy. I'll have to stop in now and then to see him. Or you know... if there's an hour we have still, they're going to have to clean these sheets anyway. We could do something fun."

She stopped the movement of the office chair, planting a single shoe on the ground, and met his gaze. She laughed, just a small laugh, a flash of a giggle. "Connor," she said. "I think we should break up."

She stopped speaking. He couldn't look anywhere else but at her. He wished the mattress would swallow him, but it held him up, lying on his back, on display. "But why?" he said.

She sighed. "I don't know. It's not anything you did. If you did something wrong, you know, I'd be telling you. You would have known by now. But when it came time to move out, I realized I didn't want to be in a relationship anymore. I can't save you from my gut. That's all."

That was a lie. He was imperfect, everyone knew that. Prone to daydreams, awkward in bed and in public, hard to get along with. If he was more complete she'd want to be with him. He looked at the photo of the window. What was back there, to make that color, beyond the glass, the white unknown? If he could be there, that would be better than the world he was in now.

"Okay," Connor said. "If that's what you want. But I guess, not to make you feel bad, but—I really enjoy spending time with you. More than anyone else I've ever met. So this is kind of surprising."

He wished that she had said anything about him, about herself, but she hadn't. She'd said almost nothing at all. She was the same strange someone who had shown up in his hotel room one day, not a thing about her making sense. And she was leaving, her soul going down the drain as the moments went on, and he still knew nothing of her. He didn't even know her middle name.

"I feel the same way," she said. She walked over to his bed. "Get up."

He did as he was told. She hugged him deeply, running her hand across his back. He held her close, but he only felt her jacket. It was still cold from the outside air.

"Okay," she sighed. She looked into his eyes again and grabbed his shoulders. "Remember the good things, alright?"

She took her backpack and flung it over her shoulder, and walked out the door. Connor laid back down on his bed, and rolled to one side. On her way out, she flicked off the overhead light, a habit of hers. Had she meant to do it this time? Where was she even going? He heard her jog down the creaky staircase. He listened to the front door open and shut; it was always too loud, occasionally waking him in the night. He dared not look out the window. How far was she now? Twenty feet away? Thirty at this point. She was getting further away from him, walking out of the timeline and into the blur. Into a life that had absolutely nothing to do with him.

32

C onnor slid into the booth in the diner. Pablo and Nigel sat across from him. He stared straight forward, looking at neither of them. Stirbert walked in a moment after, sitting by Connor.

"Please, a menu, please!" Pablo said, almost yelling. He looked around for the waitress. When Connor had told him the news, he'd become quite hurried in setting up the diner visit. Some food would be nice at least. The waitress walked by and tossed a stack of menus on the table. Without missing a beat, she continued out the front door and fired up a cigarette. She would often ash them on her apron, leaving little dots of black on its front.

"Strange lady," Stirbert remarked. "Doesn't she know it's cool to vape?"

Pablo waited. He hadn't bothered to distribute the menus, instead holding them in his hands like they were a textbook. The day had passed by, and it was the early night. The street lights were bulbous and white and had started to flicker on. It was wet outside, but he didn't remember it raining. Water had appeared, seeping through every crack in the pavement, every gap in the concrete, and puddling in every depression. Slick with the oil and crud that was buried in the road surface, it would stick to his shoes and follow him wherever he went. It would drip from the rooftops and the leaves of the dying street trees. Slick and viscous and unseeing.

The waitress returned. "Four milkshakes, four stacks of waffles," Pablo said. "A side of hash browns, a side of French toast, a hot chocolate. Please and thank you."

Nodding in wordless approval, the waitress left. Pablo extended both his arms outward, in the way he did sometimes, and sighed. He put his hands both flat on the table, pressing his fingers into the wood. "I felt a most terrible disturbance today," he said. "I felt as if hell came to greet me earlier than expected. So I did the natural thing and asked you to come here. I'm sorry, my friend. I'm just blabbering at this point—it's a difficult thing."

Nigel gave Pablo a knowing glance. "So, what happened?" he asked. "Did she just up and leave?"

The door swinging shut in the hotel room. Her boots walking down the stairs. "Yes, basically," he said. "She said she just didn't want to be with me anymore. Said I didn't do anything wrong. I don't know."

"There was nothing wrong? No sign at all? I thought you guys were great together." Nigel asked.

"Hey, give the kid a break," Pablo said.

The way she pinned her hair up that day. The way she looked at him. The way she wore that sweater she would never wear. The way they'd failed to accomplish what they wanted.

"No, there was nothing," he said. "I mean, a bad thing happened. It really sucks that we didn't get the result we wanted. She was upset, is upset. I am upset, too. But I didn't think she'd leave me. It wasn't my fault. We got along great. Things were great. I guess I thought we needed each other. That a hard time might bring us closer. But that's just dumb, I guess."

Pablo rubbed his hands together. He looked down at them, and back up at Connor. "She was a strange girl anyway," he said. "You must not worry about her. You can't understand someone like that. You can only observe. If she's not mature enough to talk to you about what is in her soul, well, you don't want to be with her anyway. Me, I bear my soul perhaps too often to these women. Perhaps that's why I'm alone. But I do it just the same because it is the only way I know how to live."

"I don't know if that helps," Connor said. He got along just fine with her.

"Well, you have us," Nigel said. "Either way. We won't walk out on ya."

"It's hard to shake you guys," said Stirbert.

Nobody talked for a few moments. Connor's body did not feel heartbroken. It felt nimble, hungry for a meal, ready to go back to that hotel with a clean bed, where he might see her again. He looked at the last text from her on his phone. Something mundane, coordinating with him about the boxes they needed for moving out. He was so hungry. His stomach groaned at him.

The milkshakes came out first, along with a hot chocolate. Pablo thanked the waitress. He took a long sip of the hot chocolate, draining a third of it. He then turned the milkshake upside down, shaking much of it into the mug. He stirred the concoction with a spoon.

"Here, try this," Pablo said, pausing when he saw Connor's reaction. "Well, you'll have a sip, at least!"

Connor had a sip. It was very sweet and chocolatey, but the texture was poor. "It's alright," he said.

"It's alright! Alright, whatever, fine. No milkshake reviews today."

Connor was not in the mood to provide a milkshake review. "The tasteful thickness of it," he said, "is tremendous. The feel of the cocoa on your tongue, it dances with the milk in a pleasurable ballet of flavor. There—is that what you wanted?"

Pablo laughed out loud. "Yes, thank you," he said. "That was nice. I liked it. It's good to see you smile."

"You as well."

The food was out not long after, and Pablo readily divided the plates among the men. He often made a performance of ordering for everyone, even though he had no intent of paying for them all, broke as they all were. He liked to care for them in that way. He handed Connor the extra sides, explaining that the heart was the hungriest organ. The food was a welcome sight, and he made quick work of the eggs Benedict.

"Perhaps," Nigel said between bites of waffle, "an old English fable may be of use."

"In England," Pablo interrupted, pointing his fork at Nigel. "They have no theory. No dialectics. They only have fable. It's a mockery. But please, continue, subject of the King."

Nigel laughed, some crumbs spilling from his mouth. "Well, it starts with a frog. The frog lives a happy life in his pond, but he is all alone, so he asks Jupiter for a wife. Jupiter is annoyed with his request, but he cares for the frog, so he calls the nearest female frog to join him in the pond. The girl frog—you know, in this story, her name is Imogen, which I think is apocryphal—Imogen has never left her own pond, much like the male frog has never left his own pond. Jupiter commands her to go, so she hops across and meets the frog."

"The frog is of course overjoyed and greets her warmly. He prepares tea for her with some flies in it, the way he likes it, and gives her the best spot on his favorite rotting log to stand on. They go swimming in the pond, exploring all the cool places to do frog things like croak, and stare blankly at the humans that wander by. The frog thinks soon he'll ask her if she would like to lay some eggs—but one day, Imogen realizes something. She tells the frog that before Jupiter came and spoke to her, she'd never thought of leaving her pond at all, but now she realized it was quite easy. She'd enjoyed his hospitality in the pond, but she'd like to go visit her parents for a while, and then perhaps go see what other ponds are out there."

"The frog is heartbroken, but he's a gentleman, so they say their goodbyes, and she goes back to her old pond. The frog cries out to Jupiter, complaining how heartbroken he is without Imogen. Jupiter is quite cross, having already done a great favor for the frog, which it seems to have squandered. He says to the frog, go mind that business and sort it yourself. So the frog hops off in the direction where Imogen went and finds a nice-looking pond, much like his own. And he meets a nice girl frog, one who prefers remaining in her own pond. Her name is Margaret—she is Imogen's sister. And they all lived happily ever after."

Everyone sat silent for a moment. "There's actually no way it ends like that," Stirbert said. "What was the point of the story?"

"I'm not sure," Nigel replied. "It's just a story."

"Aren't fables supposed to have a lesson?" Stirbert asked. "The lesson here is, as far as I can tell, if a girl rejects you, shack up with her sister?"

"Not bad advice," Nigel said, sipping his milkshake.

"Just don't listen to him," Pablo said, waving his hand in front of Nigel to block Connor's view of him. "He's gone completely insane. He's not to be listened to. Telling nonsense stories like this. I have something much better for you—a proverb."

"A proverb?" Nigel laughed. "Well, certainly the wisdom is more concentrated in a proverb than a fable. Let's hear it."

"Yes, indeed, that's a great point, Nigel," Pablo replied. "Condensed wisdom. It is like condensed milk. Yes. It goes like this: You can give a mouse a cookie, but you can't make it drink."

"I think mice can drink," Stirbert said. "Can't all mice drink water? They need to do it to live. They're living beings."

"It's a proverb! It's a proverb," Pablo said, annoyed. "It's not meant to make sense on the first telling. Plus, I believe there is a translation issue from the original Russian that we are missing."

"It's a Russian proverb now?" Nigel asked.

"Yes, I believe so—perhaps Belarussian. Let's hear it again: You can give a mouse a cookie, but—and this is the most important part, listen closely—you can't make it drink."

"I just can't help but feel like you have that one wrong," Connor said. He pushed the remaining hollandaise sauce around on his plate. "Maybe I've remembered it incorrectly, though."

"Oh, so he can speak! And he knows proverbs," Pablo replied.

"What would be, in your infinite wisdom, the correct interpretation of this proverb?" Nigel asked.

Pablo cleared his throat and set his utensils down. "It's quite simple. The only thing on the mind of a mouse is to eat. The mouse will happily take a cookie. Now, this is a design flaw by the mouse's creator, for eating can make you very thirsty, but the mouse is so ravenous as to forget that fact. So, as someone who cares for the mouse, you bring it a thimbleful of water to have, to keep it hydrated. Yet, the only thing the mouse wants is another cookie, so it will ignore the water, and then die. We are all just mice, my friends, with a burning wish for more cookies. Cookies are all we think about. But it's the water we need, and we aren't smart enough to see that."

The bill came. Nigel picked it up and squinted at it. "Don't worry about this one, Connor. And Pablo? I'll have to decide if that was profound or stupid."

"Maybe a bit of both," Connor laughed. Maybe if he loved anyone at all, it was his friends and their antics. He had never cared much for cookies.

33

The painters walked down the street, single file. The money had run out. It had run out long ago. It was time to get back to work. The familiar brick sidewalks and lowrise commercial buildings greeted them as they walked, as they always did. They were happy to wear the jumpsuits again. Pablo had insisted they splurge on some new ones, and that they did, their white outfits reflecting the cold morning sun.

Connor held a bucket of white paint in his hand, the weight hurting his shoulder, having already walked a mile. The ache was something he'd quickly get over, as he started working again. The railroad had been repaired—one of the first things to get done as part of the rebuilding effort. There had been some protests, but it was too important of a corridor to have it removed. The hastily reconstructed trestles, fences, signal boxes, and other bits and bobs needed a fresh coat of paint, something they were happy to provide.

They had actually been at the diner, again, when Stirbert had gotten the phone call. He'd placed the phone on speaker and set it down in front of them. His father, sounding apologetic, had said just one sentence: There's work, if you want it. Pablo cursed the betrayal of his values, Nigel hemmed and hawed in his own way, but they'd all agreed that they needed to get back to work. They told Connor it would be better if his mind were occupied.

That familiar and strange feeling came to Connor again as he reached where the sidewalk ended. They ducked, one by one under the caution tape, onto the gravel. It had been so long that the dusty, flattened neighborhood had developed its own peculiar microclimate. There was the playa, the flat and hardened area of dirt where the rain sat on top and wouldn't soak through. The piles of trash and burnt-out cars that had collected some of the sand and dirt that had blown around, sprout fast-growing weeds and saplings, islands of twisted metal with blooms of green under the sun. A few dry streambeds ran from high to low areas, depositing gray and polluted alluvium as they cut shallow veins through the dirt and gravel.

Some shady spots had piles of beer bottles, cigarettes, and empty vape pods, places the teenagers had found or fashioned for their own escape and amusement. Nigel fired up the speaker that hid in his backpack. Some soulful indie rock, some classic Junk from a decade or so ago, began to play. The music echoed over the land as they set their tools down by the tracks. There was a new signal box and a maintenance shed, both of which needed a fresh coat of paint. It was the first of many small tasks for the day.

Connor made quick work of the signal box on his own. The metal resisted the bristles of his brush, forcing him to press into the material as he made his strokes. There was no rust; the box was brand new, its surface gray and featureless. It was odd to imagine this work translating into money. Just sitting here, with his bucket, doing this simple task, was guaranteeing a future direct deposit in his bank account. More money than you could ever really hope to make when making art, singing, writing books, acting, or anything worthwhile. Connor felt lucky that he was no good at any of those things, so he didn't regret that fact as much as some other people did.

As he finished with the box, he looked down at the trowel in his hand. What mark to leave behind? He had his own, but it had fallen out of use in the months he'd been out of work. The whole thing was silly, anyway, but it was good to leave a sign that you'd been there. Make ninety-nine percent crap, Pablo had once said, and one percent art. And the art will critique the crap automatically. He bent over and picked up a handful of the gray fill that surrounded the rail bed. He took a dip of paint on his trowel and mixed it in with the sand. In one stroke, he scraped a square, slightly off-white in color, tilted to one side, into the finished paint. He backed away, satisfied with his work. It was only visible from a few feet away.

The real construction had yet to begin. The railroad, being a single vein of a great nervous system, was the first to rebuild. The architects for the main project were slow, and the cost was spiraling higher as time went on. Occasionally they'd see a few bulldozers, rearranging land, leveling it, grading it. Sometimes surveyors would bring their tripods out, wearing hard hats and high-vis, simply because they had to.

Their favorite worker to talk to was the geological engineer, who came driving a strange truck with a large drill attached. He would park it somewhere, the location seemingly random, and drill a hole deep into the soil, 'to find me some bedrock', he'd told them. He was great for conversation, and they'd offer him some cans of Boom when they saw him. He said that sometimes, when work was slow, he'd deliberately drill in a spot that would yield bad data, so he could get paid to come out the next day and try again. He said that after a while, you knew just by eye what readings you'd get. He really cared for that drill. He'd lay his gloved hand on the hydraulic arm as it dug into the soil. He wanted to 'feel the hum', he said. He said it told him everything he needed to know.

The days had begun to grow darker and shorter. One day on the way to work, Connor sat his bucket of white paint down on a place in the middle of that gravelly place. He sat there and thought of the things that he had already thought too much of already.

This was a special spot to him. He had pored over an old map, traced his steps, closed his eyes and walked, trying to remember something—his old apartment. He was sure that this was where it was. He remembered little now of how it really felt to live there. He knew where he kept his books, where his laptop was, the way he'd arranged his desk, but the feeling was already lost to him. His memories had a way of losing their feeling the further away he got from them.

He looked out at the tundra. A pair of diggers were making a path for a storm drain, channelizing the flow of the little stream that had sprung up after the land had been cleared. He tried to imagine the old view out of his window from this spot, the maze of buildings and trees stacked on one another, the forest in the distance. The trees were still there, past the burnt meadow by the river, but not much else.

The guys had different ways of explaining what had happened. Nigel would say she was just peculiar in general, that something was bound to happen. He said that applied to the old neighborhood as well. Pablo would mention a time where she'd said something cruel, claiming she had a dark heart. He said that the affair made him realize that many people in the city may have deeply flawed souls and that they did not want and maybe did not deserve good things.

He regretted how easy she had made things for him. He couldn't remember ever being strangers with her until they'd broken up. Things had never been awkward. She'd just walked down the hill one day, and things quickly went into full swing. Pablo, in one late night they'd spent drinking together, had argued that this was what had scared her the most. To wake up one day next to someone you cared for and who cared for you, having been unprepared to think and be with someone in that way. That was enough to send someone running the other way.

In the near distance, a permanent memorial was being raised. A series of stone obelisks, one for each person who perished in the fire. It was a stupid kind of way to do a memorial, very overdone, but he couldn't bear to see it. There was a lot he had refused to see, and this was one of them. If he thought about it, he remembered the field hospital that had sprung up across from the McDonald's, when its flag still flew at full mast. There were missing person ads for people that were likely long gone. People walking around town with chemical burns. He remembered that he hadn't slept through the night when it happened. He had woken up and seen hell rain from the sky, assumed he was dreaming, and went back to sleep. There was a lot he refused to see.

He objected philosophically to being broken up with. It seemed to be a rejection of his whole self, and while he was no fan of himself, he thought parts of him were still good. He had gone around with a sinking feeling that he'd lost something. It was the feeling you got if you ever stepped off a train and realized you'd left your wallet on the seat just as the doors were shutting.

He had started to lose his sense of what he found interesting or attractive about other people because he thought of it too much. He started to focus on small things. A hair tie worn on the wrist, a strand of hair tucked behind an ear. Black leggings, and black boots with yellow laces and yellow stitching. A laugh or a smile. He ordered coffee once, and it was hotter in the coffee shop that day, and the barista was tired. As he ordered, she pulled her hair off her neck for a moment, gathering it in her hand, letting it drop as he finished articulating the exact kind of coffee he wanted from her. There was a lot he wanted to ask her about life in that moment.

The new town would start to wake up soon. The new park would have its own regulars. Some guy walking his wheezing French bulldog down an open green. Teenagers smashing beer bottles in the great parking lot. An old homeless sleeping between the stone pillars of the monument. City workers cheating on their spouses in between the rocky folds of the new government building. None of them would know exactly what used to go on there.

He wondered if she would ever be a part of the new city. There was no sign of her around town. It was like she vanished. Someone ought to have seen her by now. He figured that she had left completely. It was frustrating—her presence was gone within the space of a day. He would have liked to have her perspective on some of what was happening. She had a way of judging people and situations that he lacked. She'd ask him simple questions—Should we go out? Should we stay in? How was your day? And if the questions failed she'd have a story about some misfortune from her past. It was not the kind of thing a friend could give.

Connor picked up the paint bucket and continued on his way to work. He walked further into the wasteland that he was unable to save anyone from, serving his time, and feeling sorry for himself.

34

A mix of teenagers and young professionals lounged around the cafe. It had ceilings thirteen feet high, and musty frosted windows. Great wooden beams criss-crossed the old converted warehouse, framing the brick walls. Comfortable couches were strewn about the place, some looking like they'd been recovered from outside. Mismatched wooden tables, covered in random stickers, and clean black metal chairs were scattered around the bar. In the back of the room was a spacious stage, deserted for now, but with ample audio equipment attached.

Leaning against the bar, which had a dark wood counter with clean white tile beneath, was friendly old Steve Balboni making coffee. He smiled as he took instructions from a young professional for yet another oat milk latte, which he was delighted to make. As he gave her the coffee, he told the young professional about the need for more female editors on Wikipedia, and how she could make a real impact there, if she wanted. She smiled politely and brought her coffee over to one of the nearby tables.

Sitting across from her as she took her seat was Stirbert, wearing an uncharacteristically nice sweater, and clean jeans. He smiled and placed one of his hands on hers from across the table, and she eagerly accepted. Pablo had said, privately, that while he was 'proud of the kid', he didn't know if he could have his own heart broken by seeing a relationship falter, and would have liked if they all stayed single. At the very least, they'd all agreed she wasn't invited to the diner straight away. He also remarked that while Stirbert was the closest of any of them to being a young professional, having a college degree and all, he thought that the gang had roughed him up enough that no woman like that would realize they were from the same social class. She was made up well, a lab rat of some kind, the kind of girl who wore those chunky gold earrings and didn't own any pockets.

At the far end of the space was Nigel, sitting behind a counter on a tall stool. A few young professionals were sampling paint swatches, as he pattered on about color theory, the differences between certain shades of white, and the weather. There was a tremendous shelving unit behind him, with a colorful array of paint and other goods for sale. A rack of used white jumpsuits were for sale, the white splashed with a dozen colors of paint each. which a few teenagers were picking through. They were arguing amongst themselves, trying to decide which ones looked more worn out, more indie. That one had been Connor's best idea—all they had to do was take some old paint buckets, pour them on the ground, and then roll around for a bit. That doubled the resale value of the jumpsuits.

At the back wall, behind the stage, Pablo was perched up on a ladder. He was three-fourths of the way done with a wide mural. It depicted the west end of town, as it once stood, to Pablo's memory. It was not exactly true to life—warm orange light poured out of certain windows, streaks of blue and white littered the sky—signs of life, Pablo had called them. Some buildings swelled at the top or twisted left and right as they grew. Dozens of tiny people were painted on the streets below—some had two heads, or three arms, or no legs. Everyone said it was his best work yet; it invited you to stare, trying to understand what he meant. For Connor, it filled him with nostalgia, for he also remembered it as a twisting, burning place, full of life and odd people.

Pablo insisted on having no stake in the business, but they had still agreed to fund him well since he did as much work as anyone. It turned out to be a good thing, since his mural work, while only halfway done, had attracted the attention of a wealthy client, who wanted an expansive mural of his own. He was on his way to being a working artist, while still being able to pick up shifts at the paint counter if he needed to.

Behind a door labeled 'Employees Only' was a well-appointed living room. It had photos of various bands lost to time, printed sections of vintage maps of lost places, and an assortment of fake plants. In the corner was a cat tree, an orange cat lounging at the top level. A torn oriental rug sat on the floor. On the couch was Green Gary, laughing as he spoke to Stirbert's father. Stirbert's father (also named Stirbert) was an older man, with a cold face that was a lot less cold when he was laughing. They had gotten distracted while poring over a pile of papers and were trading stories about business. When they'd all come to Stirbert Senior with the idea for a coffee shop, Gary was who'd impressed him the most—his business acumen, his slickness, his candor.

Connor swiped a note that waited for him on the counter. Eggs, three dozen. A package of sponges, at least six! No less! Salt. Apple turnovers, you know the ones I like. Gary had a peculiar way of writing a shopping list. He stuffed it in his pocket and swung the double doors open to leave. They had been worried about the location—this place was outside their usual area. There were the parts of the city, while not traditionally part of the west end of town, that came close to its character and density. Those places could be pretty expensive. They wanted a place that the 'real people could hang out at' as Pablo had said. That left the most decayed part of town, a place ravaged by deindustrialization and suburbanization, forgotten to time. There were handsome brick industrial buildings, cinderblock landscrapers with tall windows, and empty, cheap spaces, looking for any tenant that would move in, whether that was an adult video store, a weed store, or a coffee shop.

But between the brick buildings was wastage. Parking lots fenced in and over-grown. Scrap metal yards of suspicious character. Railroad tracks to nowhere, sections twenty feet long sticking out of the ground like splinters where the pavement cracked and fell away. Exhaust fans, chillers, air handlers, true antique equipment, rusted and leaking all over the sidewalk. Maintenance men milling about and looking at you suspiciously when you were on your way through. It was the kind of place that people warned each other not to go, for no reason other than rumor. There wasn't even anything there for criminal elements to do here, so they didn't go. Gary had had a bold prediction: If it all goes right, he'd said, everyone will want to live here. This will be the spot. Things would change very quickly, he said. It'll outgrow us, even the first ones to try it. Connor thought he might be right. Graffiti had begun to sprout on the facades of abandoned buildings and on the abandoned park cars. The slow hum of the city had started to extend there.

The cool and the young had this place on their radar—partially thanks to some heavy marketing led by Gary, and the shows he'd book there. They were happy to keep the place open late if a good enough band came by, and there weren't any neighbors to complain about noise. A burgeoning scene was growing around the cafe.

What Connor liked the most is that he felt some ownership of it, beyond the monetary. The concert was great, and he had his role to play in that, but he was backseat to Gary, his old girlfriend, and whatever other things he had to worry about. Always worrying. The coffee shop required much more work, more than he could have imagined. He liked doing odd jobs like shopping, unclogging toilets, and haranguing the landlord on the phone when the compressor on the condensing units broke down. He had a serious role to play in making it function.

Setting up the space had been tremendous fun—they had all added something of their own to the space, but still asked for the others' opinions: If I brought this orange couch in, would it clash? What do you think about this paint color for the back wall? Should the stage be a foot high, or two? There was power in getting asked for his opinion that made him feel more like he existed, like he was more than just a pile of pain receptors vacuum-sealed in a meat package.

A blue jay perched on a power line that sagged far too low, and gazed at him. He could never decide if the way birds looked at you was dumb or intuitive—either way, they couldn't speak English. The warmer weather had brought the birds back. How silly it was, really, to feel a bit better when the sun was out. It was the kind of thing you heard thirty-year-olds talk about—but then again, maybe he was getting old.

35

Connor swept the floor as the sun set over the city. He gathered straw wrappers, crumbs, dust, and anything else that fell on the floor. Everyone else had gone home, it being an hour past closing time, but he liked to take time to clean when he had the energy. It was a light that they only saw on the days they closed late to have a show; the orange light of the sun closing out the evening, bathing the space through the frosted windows of the old warehouse, casting long colored shadows on the room, and on himself. The cleaner he could get the floor, the more the sunlight would shine. The light of this day was especially beautiful.

The weather had been kind to them lately. Bad weather days were bad for the shop, since most of their clientèle had to walk a considerable distance from where they actually lived. They had made a couple regulars out of those who did live nearby—the scrap yard manager, who ended up being a nice guy, always asking if they had any metal objects they didn't want—and a homeless man who lived in the scrap yard, who they'd give old croissants to at closing time. Connor was pretty sure the two didn't know of one other, and he wasn't about to tell.

The door swung open. Connor jumped, still holding the broom. Walking in the door was Vincent Reznor, who had the fame of being arrested (and apparently released) for that incident at the governor's press conference. He looked around, and took his flat-brim hat off, holding it against his chest solemnly.

"Hey man," Connor said. "We're closed."

"Yo, I thought there was a show tonight?" Vincent asked. "At least that's what I thought. Where is everyone?"

"The show is tomorrow," Connor said. He put the broom down and walked over to Vincent. "We close kinda early when there's no show. Sorry."

"Damn," Vincent said. He looked around for a moment. He looked like he did that day. The same cool dude, somewhat sunken, somewhat worse for wear. He had a white tee on and some baggy jeans. His beard was trying hard to grow in.

"Do you want a snack?" Connor said. "I was about to toss some of the pastries. Let me look."

He found a tray of almond croissants and put it down on the table.

"Damn, thank you," Vincent said. He sat down and began to eat eagerly. "And you guys just throw these out?"

"They don't last so well overnight," Connor said.

"I guess so. Thanks, brother," he said. "Say, what's up with you, man? You seem sad. Sitting here cleaning up and shit after the place closes."

"Me?" Connor was caught off guard. "I'm surprised you'd want to know."

"I'm trying to, you know, ask people stuff shit, when I can," Vincent said. "Trying to understand people better."

"Why's that?"

"I had some bad shit happen. Man, you know all that. You've seen the news. I just want to be more thankful and shit, and be a real local guy, help people out. Well, I'm supposed to lay low. So I do that too. But it was the community that got me out of trouble. I wanna take care of them like they did for me."

"Wow," Connor said. He was surprised Vincent would tell him all this. "Well, thank you for sharing."

"No, wait," Vincent said, croissant crumbs spilling out of his mouth. "Don't pull that shit on me. What's your answer? For my question?"

"Gosh, man," Connor said. "Do you really want to know?"

"Yeah, I do."

"My girl left me," Connor replied. "It was, I don't know, eight months ago, now?"

"Are you still sore about her?"

"Yeah, I am, I guess."

"You should just get out there, man. Hit you know, some local spots. Talk to the girl working the register. Ask her to see the posters in your room—that one always works. That's the best way. Just get out there."

"That hasn't worked for me," Connor said. "Plus, you know, I was soft on her. I think I really liked her. I don't wanna use the wrong adjective, you know the one, but I was affectionate with her. She wasn't like any girl I've met before."

Vincent leaned back in the chair and looked out the window. The orange light was turning darker and lower, and it showed a scar on his chin. Connor wondered where he'd gotten it. "I might know what you mean. For me there's this girl. She's my girlfriend. I try to make her happy. But I worry all the time, and I didn't do that before. I always worry she's gonna walk out on me. I try to make her happy anyway, and hope that's enough."

"I had the same feeling," Connor said, "and then it happened. It was actually weird, the way it played out."

"Yeah, but did you make her happy? You know, there's been a few girls for me. I know maybe you are some random guy and girls maybe don't like you as much. Okay, whatever. But I don't know if I ever made those girls happy. And it wasn't really my fault, it was just my personality, or whatever, which isn't something I can change. But sometimes someone is great for you, you know, they give you all you need. Some people need something that you can't even like, put into words. Whatever it is, it isn't you. They don't know what they want or how to get it. And it makes them sick inside that you already got what you needed. Now, I'm just saying things."

Connor took a bite of a croissant. "I'll have to think about that," he said. "I don't know if it makes me feel better in the moment."

"Maybe not," Vincent said. "It's a bad old thing either way. But bad things are gonna happen to you. And they keep happening. You know, I was in an accident earlier?"

"Oh, really?" Connor said. "You alright man?"

"Yeah, it was a few months ago now. I was out on my skateboard, and I tripped over the train tracks and fell on my face. Well, next thing I know, the train goes off the rails. Boom, big explosion. I was in the hospital for like, a long time."

"Damn, that was you?" Connor said. His heart jumped at the idea. "That's crazy. And nobody knows about that?"

"Oh, people know," Vincent laughed. "I thought everyone knew. It's not my fault."

"Shit dude," Connor said. "That's some crazy stuff."

"It is crazy. I still can't even like, imagine what happened there. Am I supposed to feel bad about it, am I supposed to like, pay money? It's weird."

"It's in the past now," Connor said.

"It is in the past. See, that's a good phrase," Vincent said. "It's good for the philosophy I'm developing. I'm trying to have my own philosophy. So I can have like, a way to have an interpretation of my circumstances and shit. And I like what you said, because, I was thinking, and I realized that when something has already happened, it's like, not even real anymore. It just stops existing, because it's not what's happening right now. It's only something in your brain."

"Some real things happened," Connor said. "I mean, you can just look around. It's serious out there."

"Yeah, things got real for a while. But I'm like, how am I gonna let that affect me? Am I gonna be all weird about it? I don't know. Sometimes I wake up at night, and I get scared. It still happens. During the day, you know, I'll just hit my vape. I'll go to work. I'll hang out with my girlfriend. I don't let it be a part of my shit."

Connor looked at the empty tray of croissants. Vincent was picking at it still, grabbing flakes of bread and dabbing them onto his tongue. He wanted to be in some ways more like Vincent. He wanted to care more about the good things, less about the bad. He wanted to be the kind of guy who could eat ten stale croissants in one sitting.

"How did you get so wise?" Connor asked, smiling.

"It's funny, dude," Vincent said. "I think I never had something I needed to understand before, and now I do."

36

Four and a half acres can be covered by about nine hundred thousand bricks. Laid out end to end, these bricks would stretch for one hundred and six miles. The rain falls on these bricks, which are constructed at a pitch, the rain running over their lightly porous surface, making tiny rivers in the mortar, before being deposited into a metal storm drain of standard size and width. The drain attaches to the storm pipes that run beneath the bricks, crisscrossing, feeding one another, growing, until they deposit that water into a river.

The award-winning building rises above the plaza, above those four and a half acres. It is as if aliens visited upon the city and landed a spaceship. It is marvelous and terrible. It is art, or at least it will be seen as such, for a few years. The building is designed with offices in its perimeter, each worker assigned one window. The windows are set deep into the facade of the building, for aesthetic reasons. Some offices only receive an hour of sunlight per day. There is a courtyard in the middle, but nobody knows what it looks like.

The wind blows in from the west. The average wind speed here is higher than in Chicago. It won't blow someone over, but it will try. Walking the wrong way is a struggle. Even when the wind isn't strong, it sucks the heat from the air. It blows the rain into the eyes of passersby, onto the windshields and cars. It inverts umbrellas. It sweeps and cleans and condemns the bodies it finds.

There is no trash in the plaza. The wind pushes it along and out of sight, with its ever-present groaning and howling. A regular row of planted trees in concrete boxes have taken a permanent lean in the wind. Their leaves all point the same direction, to the east. In the winter, they shed their leaves, and the branches, spindly and shadeless, rattle against one another. Blades of the weeds that grow in the planter boxes fare better in the wind. They sway one way and another, happy to be planted somewhere, ready for whatever comes their way.

Something else roars in the distance, at the edge of the plaza. The horseless carriage, the motor vehicle. It's the middle of the day on a Monday, but the rideshare class is restless—they need to travel. One car, another. There is no end to it. Where could all these people be going, and where did they come from? They speed along comfortably, not seeing the invisible wind around them, not knowing that the building above the bricks has won awards and is being discussed in architecture schools across the country.

History groans and creaks beneath the bricks, tamed by time and memory. A history painted by color photography and by news footage, and the smartphone. Not like the old history, the one of the newspaper and black and white film and word of mouth. This one is just as durable, and that is to say that it is not at all. It looks like all the other history meted on people everywhere every day, and thus it blends into the background. A great horn sounds in the distance. The paint continues to dry, and it will crack someday, and the metal underneath will rust, and it will run red.

Also by

Brooklyn is an influencer visiting Big Bend National Park. She's beautiful, has money to spare and just the right amount of notoriety, but still isn't content. She has a nagging feeling that she's faking it. After going to the wrong party and taking the wrong drug, she wakes up deep in the desert, with no memory of why. She runs into a gang of misfit outlaws from across the border who seem as concerned with talking about their feelings as they are robbing. Brooklyn realizes she likes lawbreaking more than being an internet personality, and decides to stay with them. As she enters a world of strange rituals, nights spent sleeping under the stars, and days riding under the hot desert sun, she suspects that something about her has fundamentally changed.

Scan the QR code to visit my website, where you can find a sample of my next project, the working title of which is Follow Me Unhappy Flower.

Help me

You can find lots of goodies at my website, nicholasmarchuk.com. If you enjoyed this book, please hit my website and sign up for the newsletter. The newsletter is how I can offer people free stuff, stay in contact with them about future releases, blog, and have fun. Without the newsletter, there would be no me! I would probably fade away.

The best way to support my work is to write an honest review of what you think. Reviews are social proof that I wrote a good book, which is hard to come by. If you have something to say, say it! I am an independent author, and your voice is what can help put me on the map.

I'm going to ask you to do something else—if you liked this book, and you know someone else who might, give it to them (or buy them a copy, if you can't let go of yours)! If they enjoy it, I now have two fans instead of one, and you have a cooler and smarter friend. Both of us win. Thanks for reading! See you later.

Acknowledgements

My editor, Lesley Hocking, was an invaluable resource for editing not just this book, but an unpublished manuscript I completed with her support in high school. Her support is what made my long journey from being a random guy to an author possible.

My other editor, Helena Gill (a stylish dimensional engineer always available for a late night phone call), has long been a supporter of mine—even though she moved to Detroit—and has donated her time to this book in ways that show on every page.

My book advice group chat was very supportive. It includes Sara Holm (talented business/marketing administrator and keeper of pigeons), Amelia Sundman (my philosopher-roommate and most interesting friend), and Madelyn Margaret Battcock-Emerson (my long-suffering redhead roommate and a lover of the worse color of wine).

The cover art and design is by Ember Nevins (custom framer and future famous artist). They went balls to the wall and created a massive mixed media piece that truly stands on its own as a work of art. You can find and purchase her work at www.embernevinsart.com.

Lastly, my mom, dad, sister, and my friends have helped me be who I am today and be in a place where I can write books. I have a great support system that I have definitely put to use.

About the author

Nicholas Marchuk designs heating, ventilation, and air conditioning systems for laboratories and offices in Greater Boston. He also is an independent author of heartfelt and entertaining fiction beloved by regular people with good taste. He is a fixture at music venues, front porches, and hockey rinks, where he plays trombone with the same joy he imbues in the written word. His books record the kindness and absurdity of modern life as his characters struggle to find their place within it.

www.ingramcontent.com/pod-product-compliance
Lightning Source LLC
Chambersburg PA
CBHW050327110726
47899CB00007B/2408